WORDS MADE FLESH

WORDS MADE FLESH

TWENTY-ONE STORIES FROM
THE COMPLETE CREATIVE WRITING COURSE

EDITED BY

MAGGIE HAMAND, SHAUN LEVIN AND NATALIE BUTLIN

tree
house
press

First published in England
in 2010 by

Treehouse Press
PO Box 65016
London N5 9BD

A catalogue record of this book is available from the British Library

ISBN 978-0-9563775-2-4

Design by Raffaele Teo

Contents

Foreword

THIS SELECTION OF SHORT STORIES AND NOVEL EXTRACTS FROM WRITERS WHO have recently attended our advanced Complete Creative Writing Course covers the full gamut of genres, from detective novels and family sagas, to romance and science fiction. Serious, light-hearted, literary, mainstream and experimental, much of the work is international in flavour, with extracts set in South Africa, Hong Kong, India and Sri Lanka, as well as the length and breadth of the UK.

Many of the writers have been working with us for a year or more, often starting on our beginner's course. It is always a great joy to see these writers take their first tentative steps into writing, and then watch their progress as they gain confidence and develop their voice and their skills.

All of these writers have learned that this process takes time; that writing demands a serious commitment; and that they can learn a huge amount from listening to others' work as well as by receiving feedback on their own writing. These writers continue to learn to trust their instincts as to what they want to write and how they want to write it. As a result, the work in *Words Made Flesh,* our first anthology, has a self-assurance and a uniqueness that makes these pieces shine.

Some of these writers have already found a publisher or been nominated in writing competitions; we believe that all of them deserve to be read by a wider audience.

Rosemary Furber

from The One

I LOOK AT YOU, YOU'RE SIXTEEN NOW, THE WAY YOU LOOK AT HIM, THE WAY
you throw your arms round his neck and kiss his ear and I say to
myself, where is your fear? I have raised a girl with no fear. You
are stepping into the waters of love as if they are the finest sunlit
ocean in the world. I want to run and surround you and haul you
back to safety.

Instead I'm going to write to you, here at our kitchen table. The
place where I've written my essays, where I used to waste so many
hours working on office files, the place where I've fed and loved
you since you were born. Here I'm going to tell you about love. I've
learned a lot over this last year. I started off with the questions you
know. Was your father right to leave us? Was he right when he said
that I knew nothing about love? What was love anyway? What was
this 'falling in love' experience that our society reveres so much?
Above all, what is the opposite of love? If I knew the answer to that
last question, and could feel its truth in my bones, then maybe I
could recognise and welcome love where I found it.

So that's what this is about, Chloe. Real love. True love. Whatever you want to call it. The stuff I've discovered, that I wish I'd
known when I was your age. The secret of love.

The truth.

Where do I start? When I signed up for that course; that's as
good a place as any. Do you remember me in a filthy mood – for

a change, I can hear you say – just after your father had called from New York and I was scrolling through websites and swigging scotch neat from the bottle? Every time I thought I'd found what I was looking for, the same word stared back at me: Humanities.

Arts, we used to call it. Do you want fries with that? Well, yes. That's why I studied law. Nothing frilly or self-indulgent about me as a student. But humanities, that's human beings, the page said, 'in all their glorious diversity.' Could that mean me, too?

I was about to abandon the whole stupid nonsense when my eye caught a photograph of a man sitting on the deck of a yacht, tipping his hat at a peachy sunset. Professor Nigel Akimbola's course *Love in the West,* the website said, examines the concept of 'The One' in Western love literature from the earliest Celtic myths to the Jane Austen obsession of today. 'Is the romantic concept of The One actually viable in literature or in life?' Dr Akimbola asks. 'And does it serve any useful purpose in a mature society?'

I knew immediately that this man and I could do business.

'Charlton College,' a young male voice replied after I'd listened through the fourteen options including hash and star keys, 'purveyors of knowledge, pillage and spillage to south London's eager masses, *what* can I do for *yew*?'

'How poetic,' I laughed, 'so early in the morning.'

'It is half past midday, lady. You are born to be a student. You know what course you want?'

'Love in the West, please...'

'Love is a pest?' he said, deadpan.

''No, in the -'

'Just teasing, lady. Dr Akimbola, that one, yeah? Very popular. Very, very popular.'

'Am I too late?'

'Well, that depends. You paying instalments? We got an instalment plan, you got your bank deets handy?'

'Are they interest free, the instalments?'

'Nope.'

I'd spent most of the weekend preparing my financial forms for the divorce, listing what I earned and what Chloe and I would need in the future. Tedious in the extreme, but as I checked it through for the last time, gathered the pages and patted them neatly together, I felt impressed with myself. I could do one thing right and that was my job.

But a big payment like this could be interpreted as 'unusual and excessive expenditure' by the other side. I had to tread carefully. I breathed in and realised that I'd been treading carefully all my life. It was time for a change. I could just pay it, get it out of the way now as a lump sum and ride the storm. Otherwise I'd have to haggle about it through the lawyers.

'I'd like to pay for it all now, please.'

'You are in! Gimme your card details, lady. You are on your way to an education!'

While he hummed "You're Beautiful" and took my details, I could have told him that I'd had quite a bit of education already, but I couldn't be bothered. There was the usual trouble over spelling my name before he proceeded to my address, email, mobile number, then...

'You married, Moira?'

I reeled a bit, then asked, 'Why do you want to know?'

'Because you sound gorgeous.'

I pulled my dressing gown closer around my shoulders. Then a little smile pulled down the lower half of my face before I could stop it. When did somebody last flirt with me?

'You haven't asked for my birthday,' I said.

'Don't care. You comin' in to collect you induction pack, Moira? I'm gonna be outta here like I stole in a bit, but I'll be here again tomorrow. Till five.'

Don't care, he said. Really? Could it be true?

'What's in the induction pack?'

'Stuff about your first essay.'

Oh God.

All this exuberance was a little much for me, to tell the truth. I'd been for several hours at the laptop without food or clean-

ing my teeth. My lower back was aching and I could do with a
shower.

'I have to do an essay?'

'Welcome to academia, Moira. Studying is the name and essays
is our game.'

'What about grammar?' I said. 'Is that the game too?'

He laughed, a clear, spring-water gurgle.

'I do have a degree actually,' I went on.

He put brief details onto the admission form.

'While ago,' he said.

And there it was. The kick in the chest. Then in a small voice
he threw me a lifeline,

'I can help you if you like.'

'What?'

'I got a degree at Oxford,' he said. 'No kiddin, I can do you any
essay you like. For a fee.'

'What did you read?' I asked. I'd soon flush out this pretence
of his.

'PPE,' he said, suddenly posh. 'That's philosophy, politics and –'

'Economics, yes, I know.' He might just be telling the truth.
'And you're answering the phone to pay for it?'

'What else does a philosopher do?'

'You tell me,' I said, genuinely wanting to know.

'Life goes slowly, life goes quick,' he said, 'one thing's for sure,
sis, life don't stick.'

'Most erudite,' I said, still smiling, still testing him.

'That's pure Dryden that,' he chuckled. 'Verses to order any
time you like. So when's your birthday, Moira?'

'And I thought you were a gentleman,' I teased. 'Surely an
Oxford graduate would never ask a lady...'

'Just for the form, then I'll forget I ever knew. I promise.'

I told him the day and month.

'Last month, yeah? You's a lawyer, too, Moira, so how's this for
a late birthday poem from your friendly urban verseteer: *Happy
birthday to ya, I really wanna do ya.*'

Such elegance, I thought, but felt my face tighten in smiles again, and laughter bubbling. He went on:

'*Wanna buy ya summat new, yah*'... to a climactic finish... '*If I's a lawyer, I would sue ya!*'

The laugh burst out of me, big and belly-shaking for the first time in weeks.

'I'll take that as a compliment!' I said.

'Sincerely meant, Moira, sincerely meant. Dr Akimbola's gonna love you. He never got a student paid the lot up front before. So I'll see ya tomorrow, yeah? For yer induction pack? Don't let me down now, Moira? I'm here till five.'

I heard my own voice saying, 'I'll be there.'

I put the phone back in its charger and breathed deep into places that had been clogged tight for years. Excitement was flooding me, and not just from the random flirting of a cheeky young poet. I felt proud of myself.

It was such a little thing, but I'd done it.

I'd signed up to study love.

Laurika Bretherton
The Stakeout

IT'S EARLY MORNING, AROUND SEVEN. THE LIGHT IS CLEAR, THE SUN IS COOL. NOT that hot heat that burns you, turns your skin red, even in the shade. Kobus sits in an unmarked police car, a black Audi. All the windows are open. The radio is switched off. He needs the silence, the silence of the rocks, the quiet of the earth, the stillness of the sand. He needs it if he's not going to get ambushed today. He has a bad feeling about this one. But hell, he has no choice. He's parked his car to face the dirt road; anything coming from that side he'll see. He scans the empty veld. That big rock over there on his left? A perfect hiding point. The tree further on his right? Fuck.

What are they doing? Are they trying to buy the silence? In a couple of weeks there will be a new government in power. It's over. It's been over since that bloody Dirk Coetzee turned into a yellow canary in 1990. There aren't many secrets left. He wonders how long until his unit's secrets will be revealed. The beatings, the intimidation, the killings. It's just a question of time.

The reporters are already sniffing around. He's seen that dark blue Benz in his rear view mirror more than once. He knows it's not a cop, too much of an amateur, the way the guy always keeps a car between them, the way he backs off quickly when the car in front of him turns unexpectedly. It can only be a reporter. Who else would be tailing him? He's going to have to run the plates on that car.

Kobus looks at the clock on the dashboard. Re-checks the time on the watch on his wrist. The guy's late. Not unusual for an informant.

They're often late. Always some fucking excuse. I was sick. I couldn't get a car. He's heard it all.

He lights a cigarette, feels the smoke flowing into his lungs. The only reason for a no-show is cold feet. These guys have no pride. No self-respect. How do you sell your people's secrets for money? How do you do that?

He knows he plays a big part, a huge part, in fact possibly the only part in why they do it. They're being blackmailed. Oh, yes, they do get money, but it's only semantics, really. If they don't point out anti-apartheid agents then they'll be exposed as traitors, double agents, *askaris*, *impimpis*. Call them what you like. Their own people will kill them. It will be bloody and painful. Usually a necklace. A black tyre dosed with petrol hanging around the neck. A match thrown. Flames catching light. The smell of petrol and burnt rubber. Then, slowly, something else. A meaty smell. Burnt flesh.

He inhales the cigarette smoke deep into his lungs to drain out the image, the smell. When he started this job he was unconvinced that any one of these freedom fighters would turn on their own people, inform on them. But he was mistaken. Everyone has a button. If you find the button then you can get them to do whatever you want. It's surprisingly easy. First you administer pain, issue a few threats, break them down a little. Then once they're weak, you make some promises, promises of money, you wave enough cash before them and they'll do anything. As a last resort you use their family, a mother usually. One that sits at home in the Transkei or Bophuthatswana, who's proud of her son who's left home for Egoli, the city of gold, to make a life for himself. A son that sends money back home to buy more cows. You barely have to hint at harm to their mothers and they fold.

But sometimes, just sometimes, on a rare occasion – actually in his twelve years in the service he's only experienced it once – a man, a young man who was really just still a boy... It is a rare man who cannot be broken. Kobus couldn't help but feel an admiration for the boy. He didn't crack. The pain, the money, the threats: they didn't work. The boy's eyes silently, resolutely, defiantly, stared back into his own, right into Kobus' eyes. The others? They always looked away, afraid of what they saw. Death. They saw death staring back at them. But this guy? He didn't flinch. Didn't even blink. Just stared back. Not in fear. Not with that dull acceptance of a man who knows that he's going to die, but with a challenge. Kobus couldn't help but admire, respect him.

In the end the boy had to die. It was inevitable. You don't defy the security police and live to tell the tale. And it didn't bother Kobus, really. But he did give the boy a clean death. A warrior's death. That is the one kill he does remember in detail; one name he won't forget. Tebele Segalo. A tiny hole right between the eyes. A proper grave dug out, six feet deep. His body wrapped in a blue prison blanket.

Kobus still has the shell casing of the bullet. He drilled two holes into it and strung it through a dog-tag chain. His fingers search and find the copper cylinder lying against his chest. Yes, he remembers Tebele.

A glint reflects off his front window and he swears at himself for being so fucking stupid. He could have been killed while he sat here smoking his Camel, reminiscing about the past. For a moment he allows himself a quick thought. What would *his* button be? A pair of dark blue eyes maybe? He doesn't know. Would he face his torturers like Tebele? Fearless? He'd rather not think about it. The glint is from another car and it's moving closer. Slowly it drives towards him, disturbs the quiet. The dust begins to twirl. It's another Audi, also black. What the fuck? Did they make him sit out here to test him? He lights another Camel to steady his breathing. He looks at the person in the passenger seat and thinks to himself that maybe he'll find out today whether he does have a button.

The cold chiselled face of the Colonel. The great man himself. This is not good. No, that's an understatement. This is fucking bad. As in make-peace-with-your-maker-now bad. He takes another drag on the cigarette, opens his door and gets out. His boots crunch on the earth. He shuts his door and the noise disturbs the veld. A bird screeches and flaps its wings before taking flight.

Kobus scans the area again. The tree on his right, the big

rock on his left. The fuckers have been watching him all morning. While he's been sitting here waiting for a so-called informant they've had their sights set on him. His own brothers have been staring at him through the viewfinders of their sniper rifles. Watching. Waiting. Silently. He still can't see them but he knows they're there. The Colonel never travels with only a driver. There's probably someone lying low in the back seat, too.

Kobus watches the Colonel exit his car in a fluid, almost graceful motion. Kobus' cigarette is almost finished now. He kills the coal between his thumb and forefinger. He stuffs the *stompie* in the front pocket of his jeans. The Colonel silently follows the movements with his eyes. Kobus lights another Camel and inhales deeply. If this is the end then he might as well enjoy one last smoke. He raises his eyes to meet the other man's. The Colonel breaks the silence.

'Kobus.'

His voice is like a father, a priest. It has that same lilt at the end. That same tone of absolution.

'*Kolonel.*'

He sounds like a little boy and he squints into the sun now shining bright behind the Colonel's right shoulder. Shit, I'm acting like a *kaffir*, he thinks, as he flicks them back to the Colonel's light brown, almost yellow ones. The man not only has eyes like a lion, but he moves like one, always stalking, a dangerous man, a predator. Was there really a time when he admired the Colonel? His only excuse is that he was young, idealistic.

'I hear you have a new girl, Kobus.'

For a moment Kobus thinks that he must have misheard. Then he feels the anger starting to bubble in his gut like a hot-water spring pushing steaming liquid up from underneath the earth. It must have shown on his face, or maybe the Colonel does read minds, after all. You can't hide anything from the man.

'Oh, Kobus, Kobus.' He still uses that fatherly voice. 'All that righteous anger. That's what I like about you. You are one of my best.'

Kobus sucks on his Camel and looks into the distance.

'You know I keep tabs on all my boys. I have to know what

you're up to. So when I heard about this girl–' The Colonel stops talking. Waits. When Kobus looks back into his eyes he continues. 'See, I wonder why you haven't told anyone about her? You break off a weapon's raid to go and rescue her, like some fucking English knight.'

He laughs at his own joke, but Kobus thinks the joke's on him. Kobus should have known his actions would come and bite him in the arse. When he heard the armed robbery call on the police scanner he had to go and make sure she was okay. When he'd walked through the door and seen her crouching on the floor, fingers clenched into white fists, he'd wanted to find those fuckers and kill them with his bare hands right there and then. But there's time for that. He'll find them.

The Colonel says: 'Don't get me wrong. I'm all for chivalry. Especially when it's such a pretty little thing. But why haven't I heard about her until now?'

Kobus wonders the same thing. Why has he been keeping Fiona away from the Colonel, from his brothers? He's never done that with a chick before. Is he trying to be a better man for her? But he is a good man. He is one of the few who's been keeping this country safe.

'*Ag, Kolonel,* I've not had time to tell anyone about her. I've only met her recently.'

The Colonel's voice is cold, soft, dangerous when he says: 'I'd call six months long enough.'

Kobus decides to keep his mouth shut. The less you say the better. The Colonel smiles, showing his white canines, very much like a lion when it yawns. 'I tell you what. I'll make it easy for you. Why don't you bring your pretty little princess over for a *braai* next Sunday?'

Kobus feels his jaw tighten. His teeth nick the inside of his cheek. His mouth fills with the salty copper taste of blood. The Colonel's eyes narrow and Kobus realises that it was a test, one that he's just failed. If he'd suspected that Fiona was more than just a chick, then he now knows for sure that she is.

The Colonel changes tactics. 'Why don't you come to my

house? Let's keep it small. Just the other day Marie was saying that she hasn't seen you in months.'

Kobus doubts very much that the Colonel's wife would have said something like that; she wanted nothing to do with his boys. But it's better than taking Fiona to one of the Sunday *braais* at the barracks which usually ends with one or more naked women in the pool.

'Okay. I'll bring her.'

'Good boy.' The Colonel turns to his car. '*Kom,* Pieter, let's go. I've got a lot to do today.'

The driver opens his door and the car leaves in a plume of dust. Kobus takes out another cigarette, flicks the lighter twice before a flame springs up. He drags deep and the smoke burns his raw mouth. How many of these things has he smoked this morning? How long before the Colonel's surprise meetings turn into an execution? A bullet in the head?

He looks at the tree, the rock. Nothing moves, but they're there. He knows they're fucking watching. He turns back to his car, starts the engine and switches the radio on. He takes another deep breath and feels the air starting to flow into his lungs despite the sticky humidity that has replaced the cool morning air.

He follows the same road as the Colonel's car. In his rear-view mirror he sees three bodies walking towards the road dressed in fatigues. Two were behind the rock and one behind the tree. The one in the front lifts his hand in a fist, the sign for stop. For a moment he thinks he may just ignore it, keep driving, pretend he didn't see them. But he brakes.

He waits for them as they jog up: Theuns, Karel and Hein. Theuns gets in next to him. The other two settle in the back.

'No hard feelings, hey?' says Theuns.

Kobus shakes his head.

'Hey man, score us a ciggie. It's fucking hot out there,' says Karel from the back. His brothers. They avoid his eyes just like he avoids theirs. They all know that any one of them could be next. Tomorrow it may be Theuns and he may not get off so lightly. He may get a bullet.

After he lights his smoke Karel begins to sing along to the tune on the radio. They drive back to the barracks where Kobus drops them off. He'd moved out of the barracks into a house a couple of years ago. He and the Colonel are the only ones who live outside, in the world. He wanted space. The others like the parties, the fun. They stayed. He wanted silence. He wanted to be alone. And right now he very badly needs to be alone.

Jennifer Nadel

A Night Away

LOUISE CHANGED INTO HER WEEKEND OUTFIT IN THE LOO. OFFICE GREYS TRADED in the unkind light of the basement cubicle for a black satin mini, bought specially for that night, strappy heels and a denim jacket. No time now to wonder whether she looked sexy enough. There wouldn't be a night away unless she managed to get Joe handed over. She hurriedly smoothed the fabric over her stomach and shoved her day clothes into a Safeway's carrier bag. In a second bag was a spare set of clothes for her son. Checking her watch and her tired reflection in the flickering mirror, she set off for the nursery. It was just after five. She mustn't be late.

Joe was ready, coat on and piercing blue eyes watching expectantly for her as she peeked through the glass panel on the outer door. She was always amongst the last to get there. The teachers, at that time of day, seemed too tired to keep the children occupied and so the last stragglers were left staring at the door, willing it to open. Louise had tried to persuade her boss, Martin, to let her leave work earlier but he'd said he couldn't make an exception. It would set a precedent.

It was only as Louise bent down to scoop Joe up and scour his chubby face for clues to what had happened that day that her strained expression cracked to reveal something softer.

'Come on,' she said, tucking the tired three-year-old onto her hip. 'It's time to see Daddy.'

'I don't want to go to Daddy. I hate Daddy.'

'Oh, Joe, sweetheart. You don't know him enough to hate him. Come on, let's not be late.'

Mother and child swirled in the thick of Euston's homeward-bound commuters. Louise's new sandals were rubbing and the two carrier bags had worn red grooves into her wrist.

Joe was refusing to walk. 'I don't want to go to Daddy's,' he wailed.

'I know, sweet, I'm sorry,' she said, hitching him further up her hip. 'But Daddy wants to see you. He hasn't seen you for ages. And Mummy's going away for the night. See, I'm wearing my special clothes. It's a treat for Mummy, too.'

The toddler stared steadfastly away, glum lip trembling in mute defiance. Louise headed for McDonald's, as agreed. Joe relaxed at the promise of chips and a free plastic toy. Resting him on the counter-top, she checked her watch. They were on time. She hoped he'd be.

At the plastic table, Joe sat packing and unpacking his Happy Meal. Louise took out a cigarette. Colin should be here by now. Where the fuck was he? He was the one who had demanded access. She should have just let her mum take care of Joe.

'I need a wee,' said Joe.

Checking her watch again, Louise looked around anxiously and spotted a smartly-dressed young woman in a black leather coat a couple of tables away.

'Excuse me,' Louise said. 'Can I ask you a favour?' The woman recoiled but Louise persisted, 'I've just got to take my son to the loo and I'm worried his dad will come looking for us and think we've gone. If you see a fair-haired man, about five foot nine, looking around, would you let him know we'll be back soon? He's called Colin.'

The woman nodded and Louise led Joe back across the concourse to the toilets, scouring the crowds for Colin's short stocky frame. Knowing her luck, he'd turn up at McDonald's while they were in the loos.

Funny how much of my life now seems to be spent in toilets, she mused, as she put a 20p coin in the turnstile.

'Can I do it?' pleaded Joe the second after the coin had gone in.
'Next time, sweetheart.'

Joe, inconsolable, threw himself on the floor. 'I want to. That's
not fair,' he wailed.

Louise tried to pick him up, one carrier bag accidentally slipping
down her arm and hitting him in the face. 'Come on. Have your
wee. We mustn't be too long, or Daddy will think we haven't come.'

'Its okay, I don't need a wee anymore.'

Back at McDonald's there was no sign of the woman in the
leather coat. Bitch, thought Louise, now I'll never know whether
Colin's been already. Joe slithered on and off the smooth bench.
At the neighbouring table an elderly lady tutted to her friend.

'He'll get dirty,' she said to Louise.

Louise checked her watch again. Colin was forty minutes late.
Perhaps he wasn't coming. He was making her late as well now.
She only had half an hour left. But perhaps he'd come while they
were in the loos. No, he wouldn't have just gone. Wouldn't give
her the satisfaction of thinking he hadn't turned up. He'd have
waited. He'd come. And if he didn't? Fuck knows. She'd cross that
bridge when she came to it. She certainly couldn't take Joe with
her, that was for sure.

Joe spotted a girl of a similar age in a pink dress and started
pulling coy faces at her. Soon they were chasing each other round
the eating area, creating their own world beneath the plastic toad-
stool tables. Louise relaxed into her wait. She took a small silver zip-up bag out of her black rucksack and started, as best she
could, to apply her make-up: dark wine lips, heavy on the eyeliner. She went for glamour. She needed to distinguish night from
day. But if Colin didn't hurry, she'd be late for Martin. Where the
fuck was he?

Joe's new girlfriend was taken to catch her train. Joe flung
himself at Louise, exhausted, dirt sticking to the sweat on either
side of his nose. 'I want to go home, Mum. Please, Mum. I'm tired.'

Louise checked her watch again. Six fifty-five. She'd definitely
be late now. 'How about a lolly, sweetheart? That'll help. Come on,
we'll get you a treat.' Louise picked him up. She flung the patent

rucksack over her back and slipped the two carrier bags over the crook of her left arm before setting off for the John Menzies stand. Commuters were still flowing up from the tube to stand and gawp at the board, littering her route with their suited bodies.

She hoped she wouldn't miss Colin. It would only take a minute. I'll give him till the lolly's finished, she said to herself as she handed it to Joe, then we're going. Poor baby, she thought, looking at the child in her arms. It shouldn't be like this.

Just as she was turning to leave, she saw Colin walking across the concourse. He was hurrying, but when he spotted her, he slowed his pace to a casual saunter.

'Look, Joe, there's Dad.'

Joe burst into tired tears which flowed on to her shoulder.

'He's tired,' said Colin taking a dismissive look at his whimpering son.

Louise let the bags slip to the floor. Her arm was aching. She was tired, too. 'Of course he's tired. We've been waiting for over an hour. It's past his bed-time.'

'Don't start.'

'I'm not starting. I'm just saying it's not fair on him to keep him waiting. He's only three,' said Louise, putting Joe onto the ground.

'Don't talk to me about fair,' said Colin, shoulders square onto her now, hands on hips. 'Its not fair that I'm only allowed to see him once a fucking month. Don't talk to me about fucking fairness.'

'Colin, stop. Not in front of him.'

'It'll do him no harm to hear what his mother's really like.'

'Colin, stop it or you're not having him. I'm going right now.'

'You're not fucking going anywhere,' said Colin, spitting into her face, his hand gripping her arm.

'Let go or I'll scream.'

'Oh, that'll be really good for him, won't it? To have his mother screaming like a fishwife. Glad to see nothing changes. Just get a grip, will you?' Giving her arm a shake, he let her go.

'When will you have him back?'

'When the court order fucking says.'

'Well, it said you were meant to collect him at six.'

Colin grabbed her wrist, fingers digging fury into her skin.

'Ow! Let go or I'm screaming.'

Joe was clinging to his mother's stockinged leg, lolly forgotten and head buried somewhere in the sheen of her skirt. Colin released her wrist and then bent down and slowly and deliberately prised him away.

Louise watched as her son was carried screaming across the station. She still had the bag in which, amongst the folds of his ironed clothes, she'd hidden his favourite koala. She found her arm waving in an over-emphasised arch of joviality as his head bobbed out of sight. But she couldn't feign a smile.

Soon his sobs were lost in the noise of the station. She waited just in case they turned back. But they were gone.

Outside the station where night had fallen a herd of black taxis queued in a haze of London rain. Louise weaved her way to the far corner of the car park, hesitating when she saw Martin's red Audi. He'd waited. She felt strangely disappointed. What was she doing? Why was she bothering? If only she could just go home. She should have left when Colin wasn't there on time. Should have taken it as a sign and just gone home.

She contemplated turning back, but Joe was gone anyway. Then Martin spotted her. Folding his *Evening Standard* away, he leant across to open her door. 'What took so long?' he asked, turning his Lionel Ritchie tape down.

Louise shrugged a mute reply. She slipped into the leather seat, shoving her carrier bags down beside her sodden feet. He must have come straight from work, she noted. He still had his navy suit on, though his tie was a loosened knot beneath his stubbled chin. She smelt the remnants of his familiar aftershave as he lent across and smoothed a brief kiss onto her lips before slipping the car into gear.

'I've rung the hotel. They'll keep our dinner reservation, so there's no harm done. We'll be there in an hour or so anyway. It's only in Essex. Just a shame we're going to be stuck in the traffic now.' Martin manoeuvred the car out into the exhaust-spewing queue of traffic on the Euston Road. Louise sat blankly, not even caring what the drizzle had done to her hair.

'Shame we couldn't get away earlier. Still, that'll teach me for getting involved with someone with a kid, eh?' His tone seemed well-meaning. 'I must meet him sometime. Really.'

Louise shrank still further into her seat.

As the lights changed to red, Martin turned and reached for something on the back seat. 'Here, this is for you,' he said, putting a package onto her lap. 'Thought you might need something to cheer you up.'

'Thanks. You shouldn't have,' she mumbled. She untied the shop-knotted purple ribbon and out of the black tissue paper slithered a red silk nightie with lace trim. 'It's gorgeous,' said Louise, doing her best to mimic enthusiasm. 'But you shouldn't have.'

'It'll look sexy on you,' he said, and switched the windscreen wipers to a faster setting. 'Can't wait to see you in it.'

The traffic was beginning to move again. Keeping his eyes fixed on the lane ahead, he slid his hand over to separate her legs. 'Maybe we should skip dinner altogether? No, let's eat first. Build up to it.'

Louise put her hand on top of his and squeezed it.

Satisfied, Martin let go of her thigh and shifted the car into a higher gear. 'Mmm. I'm looking forward to tonight,' he said. 'Have you brought something to change into for dinner?'

Without waiting for a reply he turned the stereo up and accelerated through the thinning traffic. 'You are my destiny,' he sang.

Louise turned her head to the water-stained window and cried silently, while outside the rain continued to fall.

Peter Miller

Rockabilly

CHAPTER THREE

Mungo's feet flopped in plimsolls. His lungs scooped in the mesh of dust and flies that floated comatose in the smog of the hot summer. He immersed himself in the music coming from the open windows of cars, feeling like a dolphin jumping up out of, and down into, the concrete crumble sea. Counting songs, singing them if he felt like it, putting on a spurt if he heard something he liked, something from last winter that had grown through the spring and was blooming in the harsh light of summer, something he didn't think anyone else liked, something he had on twelve inch before anyone else, even though he couldn't play it because he didn't have his record player at the bedsit. Never mind, he had thought, he would get someone to tape it for him, but he couldn't find anyone to do it. All that had changed, and now he was the one they were asking to tape stuff and people queued up to do him favours now that he worked in the record shop and had the DJ slot on Saturday nights and, better still, at concerts by all the bands not big enough for the Barrowlands.

The songsound now rebounding outside between buildings until the bridge let it outwards and up, filling the sky where it mingled with the slagheap haze before dropping down like dead midges to the greenery and rubble of the park below. Mungo took the steps down, leaving the cars and their stereos behind, by the teetering tower of the chip shop looking like something out of *101 Dalmatians*, down into the unwashed dustbowl of the Kelvinside

Walkway, his old route to the misery of the dole office before he descended into ME inactivity and his subsequent fallow period, the scraping clean of his blackboard.

His footfalls echoed in the malodorous tunnels, the whole river smelling of summer rain, sharp and cool on the eyes, rubber-slapping sounds ping-ponging across then out into the deepening green that signalled the eventual approach of the Botanic Gardens.

Running full-tilt again now, he was a paper boy at the end of his round, trusting he would not encounter any dog walkers or lard-arses round the bend. Up and up the tiny steps, away from the river and its vague tributary tang of sewage from the tower blocks that abound upstream, up and out and into the open to gaze with ruddy cheeks and sodden bowl-cut hair upon the mass of people lolling on the glasshouse grass, traffic moans and hums drifting back through the low-intensity chatter and circling the Victorian splendour containing hissing palms and lily pads.

He stopped running, hands on hips, then leaning down, hands on knees, touched his toes, because he could, and this was an unusual ability in Glasgow – it got you some props from the girls. He took some time to catch his breath. That last climb was always a killer.

He knew Lena would be here because she'd said as much to Ray and he'd overheard, and he knew he would find her, because he always found whoever he was looking for and he always would. Well, this was the first time, but even so. He was high on running and this would transmit itself to her and she would be intrigued because he was a runner, not some blubbery oaf. She would talk to him about music, he would not bore her and she would not be bored. Bands have their pictures taken here, he would tell her, you see them on the backs of albums across the years and across the subcultures: punkers, poppers, sixties obsessives, new wavers, no wavers. Everybody came to the Botanics because it looked good and because the BBC was just across the way and they all hung about at the BBC hoping for some kind of break that would or wouldn't come, but they would all end up sloping off across the road and through the massive sandstone gateposts and into the Botanics, which is like a kind of wonderland compared to the streets that surround it.

All the bands had the same idea, that a photo here would look great on their record sleeve, the record they hadn't made yet, the record that would enable them to laze around here all day every day, or leave for good, upwards and onwards, to London, to New York, to Los Angeles. Mungo liked it here; everyone liked it here. People's pulses slow down and as their eyes get used to this weird outcrop of natural things they start to notice the leaves and flowers and begin to appreciate the edging and the shadows or the dew or the rustle of the city breeze or, if it's hot and busy, the baking bodies sprawled and lolling, siphoning off their natural pastiness into the carpet of daisies, the drinkers and the ice cream vans.

In amongst the trees, a big ironrust manhole lay coiled and ready for kids to lift off the lid and clamber down into some kind of subterranean chamber, God knows what for, but it had been on the telly. They'd had some bands down there and set it up for filming. BBC Scotland had done it, it was always BBC Scotland, big letters in the background, refracted through the glasshouse. It was like they had spread underground from their headquarters over the road and now they were trying to come up and take over the gardens.

But everyone forgot about these underground chambers except Mungo and Ray – they had done their best to find them but they hadn't managed it so they thought maybe the BBC were just making it up, some joke, and really it was all filmed in the studios with some strange unearthly lighting to make it look like sunlight filtered through grilles way above the band members' heads, making them look holy or beamed down. Mungo wanted his band to play there, so he needed to find the way in. Ray had helped. Ray had been the one to find the manhole cover, yelling, "Raised ironworks!" when he tripped over it and barked his shin on a tree. But it was rumoured that there were tunnels all the way from here to Kelvingrove Park and that the acid heads went down there tripping off their skulls to freak themselves out a bit more, to get better value for money.

Trouble with all these people about is getting in amongst the bushes without looking like you're going for a slash, which isn't the done thing, even in Glasgow. Not in the West End, anyway.

Mungo couldn't see Lena, so now he had his breath back he started to zigzag down the slope, keeping his eyes open for ponytails and quiffs and skirts spread out wider than picnic blankets. And there she was, sitting in the shade of a huge monkey puzzle tree. They were from Argentina, monkey puzzle trees. Mungo had read the label before for some reason. So here we had a Northern European beauty dressed in North American clothes from thirty years ago poisedly reading what Mungo imagined to be French Literature beneath a South American tree in the West of Scotland. Mungo's mind was blown.

But when he got closer he realised it wasn't Lena at all. His mind quickly de-blew itself and he veered away towards the gates and Byres Road. But then he turned, went round the back way, circling the green expanse and the patchwork people, gazing at the girls through leaves, breeze and sweat and instability, his shins feeling brittle, bark-bitten, and there were dappled bits of grass and mulch under the trees, shadows like musical notes.

Neatly labelled trees. Everything in order, but the notes tumbling around each other. Like his records in big plastic crates so he could haul them downstairs to the taxi when he was DJ-ing on Saturday nights. A tenner here, a tenner there, and all the chatting-up he could handle, that was his reward. Colour-coded crates. Ray helped him shift them, then sat on the table all night drinking and moping. About Lena now, but before her about some other girl. Always one or the other. To take Lena away from him would be easy. Just to borrow her for a bit.

Mungo did some self-satisfied stretches and then started trotting again, this time up the hill, heading for the sky, till the tower blocks came back into view through the trees and tenements. Out of the Gardens and onto the streets. The kerbs were so high. Hoof-clopped carriages were once commonplace here; now just puddles and parking prevailed.

Along, along and head out west, Anniesland and beyond. He could feel the call of the canal now. He would head up there when he was far enough along and run back along the dank and dreary towpath. But today was a beautiful day, maybe even the canal would look nice. Leave the boys behind. A battle to the death between glorious sunshine and derelict canal scum.

Heaving up the hill now, hospital at his back, Mungo started to feel the strain on his calves. He wondered why he was so keen on nicking his best friend's bird. Did he really like Lena? Not ever so much. The thrill of the chase? No, not a chance. Just for a laugh? Yes, that would be it. Just for a laugh. Same as everything else. Stave off boredom for another decade or two. She would be a lucky charm against bath chairs and ear trumpets.

All Mungo's hopes were centred on the group. To get in there, make a record, bash one out and then play some gigs. Not big ones, just some down-at-heel shindigs, brash and noisy.

Turning onto the towpath now. Deeply rutted by pram wheels, buggies and BMX bikes. The mud a toxic colour and seeming to ooze from bank to water, rivulets of piss wriggling like elvers, strips of saturated toilet roll streaking across the towpath and bundling up around twigs. A smashed sewage pipe. The smell was retchworthy and Mungo tried to skip through the effluence, protecting his plimsolls. Fat flies drowsed into him. It was impossible, his skipping game, so he started to wipe the slime off on some long grass, but the long grass was full of dogshit anyway. This place was pretty much top of the pops with dogs now, and the flies just swooped into their slipstream.

Mungo wished he had his dictaphone with him now because he could feel a song coming on, a kind of 'Dark End of the Street' song, only a bit lighter, a bit funnier, a bit less existential. Less hellfire, more hula-hoop; that was his approach to ripping off the entire Soul back catalogue and turning it into slow-drip treacle to clog up the charts in his mind, made-up charts that he kept updated on his wall using a converted league ladder out of *Shoot!*, the team names pasted over with pictures from *Smash Hits* so Dundee and Aberdeen represented Howard Jones and Nik Kershaw, while Stenhousemuir masqueraded as The Thompson Twins.

Perhaps he should just leave Lena alone, let Ray get on with digging his own hole. Maybe he could have just one quick go on her, assuming she'd let him. And he did assume this. He was absolutely certain he could charm his way into her elasticated affections, if only temporarily. Ray usually got entangled with girls nobody else could ever possibly like. Whether this was by accident or design, Mungo had no idea, but it had always worked out that way. And from this Ray had suddenly graduated to going out with a near-perfect girl whose only flaw was a boyfriend in prison.

Mungo heaved himself up from the towpath and onto a knackered bridge, half of its bricks stagnating in the canal. He crossed it and found himself on a plateau of wasteland overlooking Glasgow. Smog hung like unwashed net curtains over the mass of buildings.

Parched now, Mungo was as unused to the heat as was the city. Up here the houses were of the shoebox variety, a world away from the tenements below. People slept here, had kids here, did their shopping here, but they worked in the city and had to get around on big orange buses unless they had a car, a spluttering Vauxhall Viva. Colours were dull, fighting with the grey of the usually overcast sky. Buildings crouched in shame below today's expanse of blue.

Mungo stood and surveyed. He needed a drink. He could see a newsagents with a Wall's ice cream sign outside. They would be raking it in today. But not from Mungo, he hadn't brought any money with him. Or his beloved bus pass. He hadn't intended to run this far, his thoughts had blinded him to the distance. Water water everywhere, but full of rats' piss. He could either turn back or plough on into the lair of the smog monster. That's what he would do, swing round through the city centre, past the bus station, check out the times. He thought Lena had gone home to the coast for a few days, perhaps she would be coming back. Perhaps she would want some help with her bags. Mungo thought he had overheard this plan at some point, a muttered aside or a plastic shard of conversation between Lena and Ray. The idea solidified in Mungo's head. It slowly became baked as hard as the bricks at the bottom of the murky canal, then split into a thousand stones in his shoes.

Having stopped for a while, his calves had seized up like a cement overcoat. As the sweat dried on him and gave him a memory of being cold, a ghostly request on the radio, a reminder of how it felt to have an ice-laden drink in his hand, he began to hobble across the waste ground in the direction of Killermont Street and the city bus station.

Rochelle Gosling

Macaroons

MOSES PETER SEPTEMBER MAWENGU HOLDS THE STIFF WHITE CARD TO HIS NOSE and breathes in deeply. He runs his fingers over the gold emboss-ing at the top – 16, rue Royale – 75008 Paris – and then uses the card to fan himself in the forty degree heat. Adjusting his position on the old ten gallon drum, he gently lays the card on his lap and slowly slowly draws concentric circles around the little gold sticker holding the white box shut, round and round as though an incantation or prayer.

'It's too hot. I won't open it here. I will take it to Mama Tembi-sa,' he says aloud to no one in particular. It's only ten in the morn-ing but the cicadas are already in chorus with frenetic intensity.

Later, sitting at the faded red Formica table in the cool of the Mazawattee Tea Palace he watches Mama Tembisa sweep the dust out of the front door in sudden bursts of haze. It seems to him that most of it is blowing back inside but Mama sweeps on relent-lessly, clucking as she does so, the sway of her ample hips almost hypnotic, punctuated by the movement of her buttocks like two cats fighting in a bag.

They are alone; most customers arrive closer to midday.

Without turning round she speaks into the open doorway.

'So Moses, what is in your box today, eh?'

'Ah, Mama T, today you will be tasting such love, such sweetness, you will be like the honey badger and follow me home for more.'

'*Ma Weh*, Moses, it is cake! I know it must be cake. You know I

am loving cake too much, eh? My father he was buying me cake.'
She stops sweeping and leans on the top of the broom looking out
of the doorway into the white heat. 'When I was carrying my first-
born, he came with chocolate cake from the big shop in Arusha.
Shoprite. That was before there was one here in Kirutu.'

She pauses to turn and smile at him. 'It was full of cream and
on top some custard roses. Eh, it was beautiful. The roses they
were pink and yellow and they were sweet. I was keeping them for
a long time. For the baby's christening, I was thinking.'

She clicks her tongue loudly and shakes her head vigorously
from side to side. 'But you know how it is. The mice they came, they
were eating everything, only not so much the yellow. They don't
like the yellow.' She sighs, looking back out again. 'I had no use for
them then anyway. It was better that the mice came. I think so.'

She starts sweeping again, this time pushing the broom along
the grey cement in long smooth strokes towards Moses' table.

'Show me your cake, *Baba.*'

'*Ndiyo*, Mama, this one it is not really cake. Well, I am saying it is
not like the cake you know. These cakes they call them macaroons.'

'Macaroon?' Mama extends the o, and smiles, enjoying the
sound. 'Macarooooon like babooooon. What is this macaroon?'

'You will see them now. They are small and round, crispy when
you first bite and then so creamy and so soft inside. And sweet.
But not like sugar or like honey, no Mama,' he says, sweeping his
hand in a wide arc in front of him, 'Sweet like the scent of jasmine
when the sun is setting and its nectar is weeping into the night.
The taste it is like that scent.'

Mama has stopped sweeping and her eyes are wide.

'Mama, this one is coming from overseas, it is from Paris – in
France.' he adds quickly.

'What? It is coming with the aeroplane?'

'Yes, Mama. Remember I was writing that letter to the baker
man at the shop in Paris. The shop it is called Ladureé. They are
calling this baker man *le pâtissier.*' Moses says the word slowly,
taking care to pronounce it properly, not over-rolling the 'r'.

His stumblings through the French lesson tapes which he acquired from one of his safari guests are starting to take shape, he thinks.

'I wrote a letter to Mr *Pâtissier* and I was asking him to send to me this macaroon cake for tasting. The letter it went with Mr Timothy's friend – Mr Benjamin – he posted it in England. Mr Timothy told me it was better to do this. He said the letter it would get lost if I posted it in Arusha, but if it went from London, the train would take it to Paris very quickly. And it was so fast Mama T! *Ma Weh*, I wrote it in July, and now here I have it, this box, only three months later.'

Mama Tembisa stands her broom in a corner and walks over to join Moses at the table. She wipes her hands on her short apron and pushes her headscarf neatly back into place. It had started to slip into her eyes with the exertion of sweeping.

Moses gently peels the gold sticker away from the seal and then lifts the lid of the box to reveal Ladureé's pale pink signature card underneath. He is a little loathe to hand it to Mama Tembisa; he doesn't feel her hands will be clean enough after sweeping the floors and wiping down the tables.

She doesn't touch it as he holds it out to her but fumbles in her apron pocket for her spectacles and a clean white hankie. She positions the lenseless frames towards the front of her nose and squints through them at the card. 'It is very beautiful, so clean,' she says, beaming. She reaches for it using her hankie to hold it and gently wave it in the still air, not to fan herself, but to admire the way the embossed lettering catches the light and the way the stiff card holds its form. She sniffs the air as though it were leaving a perfume trail in its wake. Moses keeps his eyes on the card. He is concerned that she will drop it and mark it forever. He holds his hand out willing her to hand it back to him, and then leans back in his chair to read to her.

'*Monsieur, it is with great delight that I enclose four of Ladureé's finest macaroons for your delectation. Please find packaged Pistachio with a fondant honey centre, Orange Blossom with elderflower cream, Dark chocolate with cherry paste and lastly, the pièce de résistance, Citron with champagne.*'

Moses pauses after each flavour as if to savour each sound as a taste on his tongue. He can smell the orange blossom, the citric tang wakes up his saliva glands. He can almost taste the almond flavour of the cherry paste, slightly warm and densely sweet at the back of his throat.

Taking a deep breath and laying the card down beside the box, Moses gently prises open the layers of creamy soft tissue paper. Each fold gives way to another, the rustling of paper packed with promise.

The paper has a soft golden sheen to it. Could it be handmade? He pauses to look up at Mama T for a brief moment. She smiles at him, willing him to go on.

Moses lifts the last sheet of paper, suddenly acutely aware of the roughness of his hands against the silky texture. The sweet smell of the fondant curls up in a wave towards his nostrils.

He stares into the box and is silent.

Inside is a harlequin massacre of smashed macaroon: the melted centres clumped together in pinks and greens, a lump of chocolate streaking the inside of the box. His throat tightens into a hard and painful knot of disappointment; almost immediately he can feel hot tears start to push into the corners of his eyes. He swallows repeatedly but his mouth and throat stay dry.

Head suddenly hanging heavy, he is unable to look up at Mama T. 'They are broken, everything it is broken,' he says quietly, whispering into the box.

Mama Tembisa claps both her hands to her face and clicks her tongue against her palate in sympathy. She shakes her head from side to side, edging forward a little to stare into the small box on Moses' lap.

He gently moves the box on the table and strokes the explosion of tissue back into it, as if it is too painful to survey, let alone taste the broken confections. He carefully folds each piece of white card into place, closes the lid, then pushes the box away.

They both stare at it in silence for a while, before Mama T says: 'Coffee with sugar and something extra?' She hurries away, returning minutes later with two large enamel mugs, roasted beans layered with the sweet smell of rum.

They sit together in silence drinking the brew. Old Jeffrey from the scrap yard down the hill makes a brief appearance. He stays long enough only to give Mama the message that her usual delivery will be late. He knows this because one of the axles to the delivery truck has turned up in the yard for sale, and these are hard to replace.

A little while later, when the mugs are drained and cold and the silence in the Tea Palace hangs heavy and deep, the multi-coloured plastic ribbon curtain hanging across the doorway parts and Sisi glides in from the heat.

She is tall; some would say statuesque, with the slim frame and long neck so typical of Masai women. 'Good afternoon, friends,' she says. 'And why does everyone look so sad?'

Moses waves the question away and, shaking his head, quickly puts the box back into a Shoprite carrier bag.

A silent note of understanding passes between him and Mama T who says quickly, 'No sadness here today, Sisi, just very good coffee. What can I be getting for you?'

'I can't stay today, Mama. I have just come to tell you that Otto's promotion came through and we are going to celebrate this weekend, on Saturday. I hope you can come in the evening?

'You, too, of course, Moses,' she says shooting one of her dazzling smiles his way.

He walks round the table to clasp both of Sisi's hands in his before saying, 'I am so happy for you and Otto, Sisi. He is deserving to be recognised in this way. You have married a good man.'

Mama throws her big fleshy arms around Sisi and squeezes her tightly. 'We will come on Saturday. I shall bring some Mazawattee Special. I know Otto he likes it so, so much.' Mama winks at them both, her voice rising in excitement.

Moses decides to walk to the nearest *dalladalla* stop, so named for the standard 'dollar' fare. It's not far and he needs the time to think.

Mid-stride he tilts his head back to take a long drink of water from the bottle he always carries with him. He swirls the tepid liquid around in his mouth a few times as though to wash away the taste of bitter disappointment. The walk is helping already. Somehow each stride forward feels like a decision in itself.

He is swept along in the steady stream of people snaking along the sides of the main road. The hum of voices and rhythm of perpetual movement is familiar and soothing. Some stop to haggle with hawkers over fresh fruit or vegetables but others hurry on their way to or from the centre of town.

Kirutu used to be described as a quiet village where a visit to the rising metropolis of Arusha constituted a major event. You could be sure that if you let it be known that you had a trip planned into town that you would be loaded with a shopping list including tea, bolts of fabric from Kaipoor's Fabric Emporium, and errands to run at the post office and bank. But now Kirutu is coming into its own. With the road leading from Arusha to Manyara recently tarred, the steady stream of safari tour operators in their regulation dark green 4x4s has led to the opening of Shoprite, a major supermarket carrying both local and imported groceries. Not many people in Kirutu can afford to shop there, sticking instead to the roadside markets, but the fact the choice is there is luxury enough.

Moses remembers as a boy coming into Kirutu on a Sunday afternoon so that his father could visit The Mazawattee Tea Palace for end-of-week refreshment. They would normally cycle in from his father's village, Moses either balancing on the handlebars when he was younger or on the bag carrier at the back when he became too big for his father to steer properly.

He wasn't always allowed to accompany his father but when he was he had to wait outside in the limited shade of the Acacia tree. Peter Mawengu was not a man who believed that children should be entertained or indulged, let alone be part of adult conversation.

Moses remembers sitting under the tree, scissoring his legs open and closed: legs closed in the cooler sand under the tree to an open-mouthed V, legs splayed in the hot sand. He would count to see how long he could leave his legs in the heat before the sand would start to burn his skin. His record was still short of half a minute; the midday sun was merciless.

Mama Tembisa seems to him exactly the same now as she was then. Perhaps she had become a little broader in the beam and a little hunched, but not so much that you could vouch it wasn't just your imagination. She must have been a very young girl when his father used to visit, but he honestly couldn't remember her looking any more fresh-faced than she did each day he saw her now.

Friday nights were the big night at the Tea Palace then. The *marogh* was freshly brewed and sometimes there would be barbequed chicken and corn. For special days like New Year or close to Christmas, a goat would be roasted in a pit near the old Acacia tree.

Moses remembers downing his first beer when he was eight. He siphoned it off one of the kegs in the back room where it was cooler, hurriedly gulping straight from the hose. He must have swallowed the equivalent of at least two jam jars because when the sun hit him, he curled up and went to sleep: the nicest kind of sleep, the kind where you feel it slowly encircle you in its arms like an old friend and you let go to sink deeper and deeper into the soft blackness of it, content in the knowledge that nothing matters more than that moment of surrender.

He is shaken from his reverie as a *dalladalla* spins into the soft dust piled up along the road's edge. The driver, who is wearing non-reflective sunglasses and a metallic red cap boasting a Boston Red Sox logo pushed back onto the crown of his head, swears at him for not jumping aboard fast enough.

The taxi is jam-packed with no seats to spare so the door has been left open for air. Moses barely has time to jump up and crouch down in the doorway facing outwards before he has to brace himself against the side of one of the front seats and the doorjamb as the taxi swerves back into the hurtling traffic of donkey carts, overloaded bicycles, pedestrians, cars and gleaming safari vehicles.

From the back of the taxi he hears a familiar voice. 'Hey, Mawengu, you don't know your brother today, eh?'

Moses looks to the back of the bus to see his friend Henry spread regally over more than two seats, beaming broadly. He is still wearing his chef's jacket which seems surprisingly clean today. The old woman next to him is sitting quietly squashed in under his armpit staring fixedly ahead. Moses notices that her head is pushed uncomfortably against the window each time Henry adjusts his weight on the seat.

'Ah, hello, Henry, I didn't see you – you are so small there.'

'What you thinking, Mawengu? You look like you are carrying

troubles, heavy like flour sacks on your back.'

Moses quickly vaults out of the taxi to let two passengers disembark and then jumps back in to slide across to a vacant seat near the window. 'It's the macaroons, Henry. The macaroons.'

Henry jolts forward in his seat, ramming his lion-sized head between the shoulders of the two women in front of him. 'They came? Did they come, Moses? Where are they? Were they good, Moses? Did you take pictures?'

'Yes, they came, Henry, with a very beautiful letter. Gold writing.'

'But what about the recipes, did they send the recipes?'

The two women turn around to cluck at Henry who is jostling them as he edges over the back of the seat with each new question. He ignores them and burrows even further forward.

Just then the taxi screeches to a halt. It has stopped at the last petrol station before the road leading away from Kirutu to Manyara. Moses' reply is lost in a flurry of disembarking passengers. A young boy has clambered onto the roof to unbundle various bags, baskets and packages, and passes them down to the line of people to find their rightful owners. This is Moses' stop, too. Henry opens the back window and leans out as far as he can as Moses steps out of the dust cloud surrounding the *dalladalla*.

In a flash of brilliant white teeth, he says, 'My friend, just tell me one thing... was there a pink one and did it smell of roses like they say?'

Just then the taxi lurches forward, throwing Henry back on to his seat. The vehicle zigzags its way through the petrol pumps before Moses can answer.

Gerda Pearce

Transkei Road

CAITLIN, LONDON

She likes September in London, the hint of winter, the crisp days, still sunny, still bright with August's remnants, just before October darkens the mornings. Autumn has yellowed the leaves of the towering trees on the banks of the Thames. They shrivel and rust, and waft their way down to the water, or to an ignoble death in the gutters. In Africa, the days would be warming now, edging nearer to a time when she would have contemplated swimming again, the days lengthening to a Southern summer. It is swimming she misses most, the languid cutting through water, her arms clearing the cool surface to cleave in, and out, and in again, the fresh feel of it afterwards, limbs trembling from the cold and the exertion. She finds British swimming baths overheated, over-chlorinated, so she has taken up running, and along the river has become her favoured route.

Today the river is full and churning, the choppy swirl of it slapping against the mooring posts, copper lion-heads now green with damp and age. She reaches Westminster Bridge and turns back for home. There is a beautiful darkening of the sky; purple clouds are full and billowing above the stoic sandstone and gothic spires of the Houses of Parliament. It is while running, ironically, that she notices more of her surroundings, that she takes in the working routine of the river, notes the shapes of the tall buildings on the opposite bank, counting the cream columns of the two that at first seem identical, only to find that they are not, the sloping limed roof of the next, with its jutting windows. Caitlin breathes in deeply and feels the ache in her ribs, the old injury playing up again, not letting her forget. She pads alongside the embankment. The orbed lamps will soon be lit for the night, but she can still make out the silhouette of her building. From the front it resembles a wave, the low swell on one side rising up to the crest on the other, with her apartment on the edge, the curl. And from the side it curves too, another wave, the illusion of water complete, given its glass exterior, reflecting the river. Her flat is on the top floor, the view high and expansive, looking over Lambeth Bridge, and not for anyone given to vertigo.

The package had arrived that morning, the courier's knock loud, invasive, unusual. Caitlin's hands had started to shake at the sight of the round, black postmark. Even the indistinct lettering didn't stop her making out the name: *Mthatha*.

Caitlin slows to a walk to cool down before she lets herself in. She leaves the flat in darkness, so she can watch the city lights wink on as she walks around, peeling off her running clothes, turning on the taps for her bath. Usually she would be quick, her mind set on the next task, but tonight something stops her, and she takes a long look at herself in the full mirror angled up against the bathroom wall. Her runs have kept her in shape, she supposes, and wonders if she looks younger than thirty-five. She always wanted to be taller, not that she is short, but it would have been empowering to be as tall as her brother Jesse had been. Her face is oval, usually found set in concentration, and she fixes her moody glare upon herself now, the arch of eyebrows furrowed into thought. A pity about the colour of her hair. Hairdressers refused to colour it, saying ash-blonde didn't dye well. She hates the grey of it, the reminder of dead fire; she tucks the thick strands behind her ears, turns off the water, and walks back into the lounge, stands naked in front of the window. In daylight, from below on the red bridge, she could peer up, make out the two floors of it, the open-plan lounge with the glimpse of white settee, the sturdy pillars holding up the mezzanine bedroom. But the rest of the interior will be lost behind the reflection, and she likes that, that from the inside she can see out, but herself cannot be seen.

The glow of the city shimmers off the surface swell of the Thames. Caitlin looks up, beyond the skyline, the domed defiance of St Paul's, the spiral sweep of black metal and blue-green glass that is the Gherkin, beyond the Eye, spinning slowly and pink tonight. Despite the threatening rain, the sky above the clouds is clear enough for her to glimpse Venus.

'Inkwenkwezi, your people call the stars,' the astrologer had said, smiling. 'And the stars will guide you.'

She had been so lost then, so far from home, so in need of direction that she had simply drifted into the woman's reception rooms. The astrologer was Zimbabwean, her accent friendly and familiar, and her kindness to Caitlin had lent the reading an air more of therapy than an analysis born of symbols from the skies. And Caitlin had thought of her father, the old man who by then was already wandering his own way, on his path into a world she could not share, as the Alzheimer's took hold of his mind, as it buffered him from the pain of his own memories.

She had told the astrologer how her father would point out the stars to her and Jesse, how on wide African nights they would stand outside, in the humming chorus of cicadas, and her father would shine his torch to the sky, pointing out Orion, his belt, and the Southern Cross. Jesse could name all the stars while she, Caitlin, could only see the blackness of the night, the shine of the inkwenkwezi, and found the torch's glare unequal to their brightness. She told the woman how she could barely distinguish the lacteal swirl of the Milky Way, but that she remembered the myth: how the Bushmen said it was ashes from the fire of the Ancients, flung into the night sky so that we can always find our way home.

London has few stars to speak of, drowned by the night radiance of the city. Caitlin turns away from the window. The parcel sits on the sideboard, contents stuffed back inside, along with the rest of her past.

She wishes her father were still alive so that he could teach her anew, so that she could learn to name the skies, to spot the Magellanic clouds, to see whether the small one was more apparent than the large, which would mean drought and bad times. But she doesn't need to find them now, to know. For there is certainly drought, she thinks. *And I am going through bad times, and I am lost. And more than ever, I need to find my way home.*

NICK, MTHATHA

He can't miss the road coming up from the coast. From Port Edward, via Lusikisiki, named for the sibilant whisper of the wind through the reeded grass; from Port St Johns, past Libode, named for a murdered Pondoland chief. But if he were headed there from inland, from the south, he knows the turnoff would hit him so suddenly, just over the crest of a hill, that he would either miss it completely or have to swerve and risk an accident. The day has been scorching. The month of the coast coral tree, *ngeyomSintsi*, ought to be cooler. He has been on the road all day, driving, the thirsty land stretching around for miles. Hills are browning with the lack of rain, and dotted with huts that glisten white against the arid day. Cattle are in their kraals, skinny with hunger.

The sky is the colour of her eyes. The sky before a storm, a moody lilac tinged with grey. But there will be no storm tonight, no respite from the heat. One of those African nights, the air so thick that one's lungs feel heavy with inhalation. One of those nights, he knows, when you toss and turn and find no sleep.

He has to swing the Jeep so forcefully it tilts despite its four-wheel drive. Nick swears under his breath. The gears grate; he grips the wheel; pulls the Jeep onto the gravelled road; comes to a halt at the side of it. Dust swirls ahead of him. The sinking sky, he notes again. The colour of her eyes.

He shifts to first, rattles the vehicle slowly up the rise of road, to where it forks. He stops again, gets out of the Jeep. His skin prickles. He can hear a chug of train in the distance, smells woodsmoke in the still evening air. A piercing call of a bird. He listens in vain for its song to repeat.

To the left, beyond the curve of hill, lies Oaklands. His father's farm. And his grandfather's before that. And once, it would have been his. If not for death, and more death. He rubs his forehead, weary now. So much death. The funeral yesterday had left an acrid taste, anger mixed with futility. He had felt compelled to go, an obligation to the girl's mother, a guilt for not having found the battered body sooner. And now another girl is missing; Vivienne's voice had been edged with a panic he dare not share. God help him, will he have to watch another mother throw soil on her daughter's coffin? Watch the earth, dry as sand, sift through the unforgiving air?

That piercing call again. No, not the rainbird. He looks down to where the sweep of wooded drive leads up to the big house of his childhood. He remembers it well, its dark cool against the relentless sun. Long cement verandahs sheltered wide windows set into thick stone walls. He pictures the rectangular kitchen with its eternal log fire stove, the vaulted front room with its stiff-backed mahogany chairs, aged Persian carpets, and austere family portraits staring down at him, his great-grandfather in starched black the most unnerving. Nick would halt his barefooted boy's run to a respectful walk beneath that glare. The dining room, with his ouma's table, carved from the *umThathi* trees that were said to have given the town its name. Laid with family silver, it was big enough for twelve, painfully reproving of his status as an only child. On the first floor, his bedroom, square and limed with white, the small latched window opened out over the eaves on nights such as this. He thinks of his mother's struggle with her English garden in the heat. The droughts and the constant need for water. His shallow bathwater would be saved for the limp roses, or the scrambling bougainvillea that housed the spiders she had hated.

Nick draws his gaze away, and looks to the right. Beyond the thin line of blue gum trees, tall and unmoving in the stasis of heat, is the train station, the post office, the trading store, the small village of Springvale. An ironic name. The fabled spring had never been found. And beyond Springvale, the house. Shandon. Green-roofed and laden with ivy. The house that held his past, and the woman who had once been his future.

Nick turns back to the Jeep. Grahamstown was always going to be too far tonight. He will find a room at the hotel. As he climbs in, he notices his boots are thick with dust. He does not bother to brush it off, his father's long-dead words echoing:

Whatever you do, Nick, wherever you go, wherever you choose to make your home, it doesn't matter. It never leaves you. You can never shake the dust of Africa off your boots.

The light is failing and he can make out Venus and the first stars, the Southern Cross. In the distance is the Matiwane, the edge of the Drakensberg. The great mountain of the Dragon. *uKhahlamba*, the Zulu say. The barrier of spears. It is a formidable horizon.

Julia Weetman

The Captain's Bar

ON CONNAUGHT ROAD, PNEUMATIC DRILLS HAMMERED, CAR HORNS HONKED, AND people carried out conversations as though from opposite sides of the harbour. Hong Kong was relentless. Arriving by air had been exhilarating. As the archipelago became visible through the clouds, the dots in the emerald sea had morphed suddenly into clusters of skyscrapers, which jutted from the land like stalagmites. The 747 swooped into its final descent, and he had stared wide-eyed as the plane soared between apartment blocks. Lines of washing were strung out on balconies so close he could have snatched at the billowing sheets. The wheels bumped onto earth, the plane hurtled toward the sea and Joe turned to his neighbour and grinned.

Isobel had telephoned him in the London flat the day before he left. She was calling, she said in a flat voice, in the hope that he had changed his mind.

Could it really be three months since he had seen her?

For a moment he wondered if this were Isobel or her ghost. He told her that he was still coming and gave her details of his arrival in the false tones of someone visiting an old schoolfriend. In a bluster of confidence, he suggested the Captain's Bar of the Mandarin Hotel for their first meeting. He clung to the safety of a public place and, were he honest with himself, he might have admitted that he hoped to impress her, that his guidebook had described the place as a haunt of the great and the good.

A doorman guided him into the lobby with the air of a palace courtier. Midday heat surrendered to air-conditioning and his feet made clipping sounds as he walked across the marble floor. A group of German tourists blocked the entrance, a stout man and three women with gelled blonde hair. Joe smiled apologetically and pushed past their suitcases. The Captain's Bar was to the right, hidden behind a heavy oak door. He heaved this open and let his eyes adjust to the dimness. The fuggy air and leather armchairs reminded him of the stuffiness of a Mayfair club and he wondered for a moment why he had chosen this place.

Only four tables were occupied - three by small groups of businessmen with silvery hair and silk ties; the other by a woman in a cocktail dress and Cleopatra eyeliner who looked dressed for a different time zone. He moved away from her and sat down at a table in the corner of the room. He had barely slept, spending most of the night staring through the window of his hotel room at the changing lights of Wanchai. When the sun had risen, bloody between the apartment blocks, he had taken the lift down to the swimming pool, and powered through the water until his limbs were ready for sleep. And so, sustained by the briefest of dozes and a flaccid croissant, he was to see Isobel again. The confidence he had felt at arriving in Hong Kong was waning. He was weary and his body harboured the feelings of a boxer returning to the ring after a lost fight. What would he say to her? Everything he had rehearsed jarred when he spoke it in his head.

He ordered a beer and stared at the door. A group of Chinese and American bankers arrived, all pinstripes and back-slapping. The tallest called for Moët & Chandon and paid with a roll of hundred dollar notes. Two women with dagger-heeled shoes claimed stools at the bar, spearing olives with toothpicks and laughing in machine-gun bursts. Joe felt underdressed in jeans. He ran a hand through his hair and looked at his watch. A first-anniversary present. One o'clock. Would she come? He reached into his pocket for the address of her parents' house. She had refused to give him the telephone number, but perhaps he could trace it.

He looked up to see Cleopatra smiling at him. She ran her

tongue over crimson lips and Joe shuddered as he took a draught of his beer from the silver tankard. He read the menu line by line and ordered another beer and some toasted almonds for Isobel. He looked at his watch again. Quarter past one. She wasn't coming.

Cleopatra lurched out of her chair and sashayed towards him with an empty glass. Not now, he thought. Please.

'Joe,' said a soft voice behind him.

He stood up. 'Isobel.'

Later, he would look at the photograph taken on their wedding day to see if she had always been so slight. She held herself stiffly, slender forearms and legs protruding from a belted trench coat. He was uncertain how to greet her and so tilted to kiss each cheek, hands skimming her shoulders. She smelt of soap and of honey and he wanted to pull her to him.

'I didn't know if you'd come,' he said.

'Neither did I.' She glanced at the entrance.

He pulled out an armchair and gestured. 'Please...'

She looked at him, as if deciding, before lowering herself into the chair. She sat upright, chin lifted and hands folded neatly in her lap. He should not have been surprised to note the absence of her wedding ring, but his heart lurched all the same.

'You look well,' he said.

Behind her, Cleopatra swayed back to the bar and slammed her glass on the counter. Isobel said nothing, narrowed her eyes and glanced down to pick a piece of lint off her coat. She had cut her hair into a bob and it framed her face in two curves of jet. He opened his mouth again, then changed his mind and turned to summon the waiter. Isobel spoke to the man in a rapid Cantonese that Joe could not follow.

'I'm glad you came,' he said. He paused before continuing. 'I've missed you.'

Isobel's eyes flicked away from him to the door and he clenched his hand beneath the table.

'How are your parents?' he asked, too quickly.

'Fine.'

'And your brother?'

'Fine.' A small sigh escaped her lips.

Barked laughter and a clang of metal sounded nearby. The bankers had sat down with an ice bucket stuffed with champagne. Each one was taking turns to stand and toast the rest of the group. As Joe looked they raised a glass to salute him. He forced a smile and turned back to Isobel. 'I hope this is okay,' he said. 'It was just a place to meet...'

Isobel said nothing, shrugged her shoulders.

'Perhaps we could go somewhere else,' he said. 'For lunch, I mean.'

She leant across the table. 'What do you want, Joe?'

'I want to talk to you.'

'We can do that on the phone,' she said. 'You don't have to fly 6,000 miles.'

'I know,' he started. 'But...'

Isobel straightened up. 'But what?'

It was Joe's turn to sigh. 'I needed to see you.' He wished they did not have to speak. He would have liked to sit closer to her, and he cursed himself for choosing this table where they faced each other like adversaries.

'So you followed me to Hong Kong,' she said. 'Just like that. No plan.'

'I've taken a job,' he said. 'On the South China Morning Post.'

'What?' she said, her face a mask of disbelief. She shook her head and reached into her bag to pull out a packet of cigarettes.

'What are you doing?' whispered Joe. 'You don't smoke.' He stopped himself. 'Do you?'

'I do now.' She flicked a white enamel lighter with her thumb and a flame shot up to light the tip of her cigarette. She inhaled deeply, tipping her head back to breathe out a narrow coil of smoke.

Joe's brow crumpled. 'In which case, so do I,' he said. He reached for the packet and took the lighter from her hand. Fingers fumbling, he scraped a freckled thumb against the flint and lit the cigarette on the third attempt. He clasped it between his lips, sucked in his cheeks and repressed a cough.

'So,' said Isobel. 'You were saying...'

Joe spluttered and wondered what to do with the cigarette.

'I'm here because I want to fix things,' he said. 'I want to show you I'm serious.'

'There's nothing to fix,' she said carefully. 'It's finished.'

'Don't say that.' His hand gripped the chair.

'What then, Joe?' she asked. 'Start afresh? Ignore the brief catastrophe of our marriage?'

Joe sank back in his chair, shoulders slumped. A cloud of cigar smoke, acrid and oily, drifted over from the bankers and he dropped his cigarette in the ashtray. He raised his eyes to hers and looked for a sign. Her pupils were vast pools in the gloom; velvet lashes blinked as she stared back at him.

'Oh, God,' she said finally. 'You're serious.'

Joe laughed. A short, gruff laugh that had nothing to do with happiness. He folded his legs beneath the table, taking care not to knock Isobel.

A waiter appeared balancing a single glass of champagne on a silver tray. 'For Madam,' he said. 'With the complements of the gentlemen at Table 4.'

Joe looked over his shoulder and grimaced. The six bankers raised their drinks and let out a whoop.

Isobel placed the glass between them and crushed the butt of her cigarette next to Joe's in the ashtray. 'I have to go,' she said. 'I'm expected for lunch.'

Joe's heart contracted as if into a fist. 'You can't,' he said. 'Not yet.'

'I'm sorry.'

'Please stay,' he said. 'Just for half an hour.'

'I can't.'

He thumped his hand on the table and the glass bounced, champagne bubbling over the rim. 'I'm an idiot,' he said. 'I haven't said anything I wanted to say.' He looked down at himself with disgust.

Isobel placed her hands on the arm of her chair and eased herself up.

'Please, Isobel,' he said, raising his voice, 'I'm begging you. Don't go yet.' He leant over and grabbed her wrist in his hand.'

She tugged her hand away, a look of distaste on her face. He was conscious of a sour taste in his mouth, of his clenched arm. He released her and stepped backwards as if punched. The image of his empty hotel room came to him, of the unpacked suitcase, the pathetic pile of photographs.

Isobel murmured something and he stared at her, silent.

She spoke again: 'Sunday.'

'Sunday what?' he asked in a tired voice.

'I'll be at the Peak.'

'I don't understand.'

'Just be there. Ten o'clock.' She paused for a moment, gaze lingering over him, then walked away; a small, pale figure fading into the shadows.

Roderic Vincent

How to Fly

On those deep dark places the conscious mind is afraid to
tread. Those are the stories we will not even tell ourselves.
Dr F. H. Syros. *The Mind Where We Live:*
Psychiatric Musings, 2001-2007

NOUGHT

I MEAN, WHAT WOULD YOU DO IF THIS HAPPENED TO YOU? KEEP IT IN YOUR
head? Never tell a soul because they'd think you were crazy?
What would you do? You don't know. Because it hasn't happened,
because it can't possibly happen. It's absurd. But what if your
life up to that point had been logical and rational and nothing
absurd had happened? What if something then happened that
you couldn't explain? Something that changed the world for you
forever. Tell a passing lover? She will leave you. Just forget about
it? The famous man's advice. Six months have passed and the
memory is no longer raw, it dissolves like smoke but the particles
are still in the air.

ONE

I stretched across the mattress to my wife, a hand in the dark,
crawling over rumpled sheets, inch by inch, slow and cautious.
If she was already asleep I shouldn't wake her. She lay still. My
knuckles arrived against the warm skin of her back. The rhythm of
her breath did not falter. I lifted my hand onto the hip. It slid into
the shallow basin of her waist and I let it rest there. I leaned in to
her neck and drew in the mingled scent of flesh and body lotion.
My lips sensed the tiny hairs.

'Bridget,' I whispered. 'Are you asleep?'

'I was.'

Silence like a block of concrete hanging over the bed. I studied the faint constellations on the back of my eyelids. From somewhere in the house came a creaking of the central heating as it started to unwind.

'What do you want?'

'Nothing.'

My hand brushed further round her waist - towards her. She took my fingers and held them. I eased myself into the centre of the bed so my chest touched her back. I stroked her shoulder and kissed her nape. My penis began to inflate against her backside.

'It's late, Tim.'

'But we said as soon as the kids were asleep.'

'You should have thought about that when you were watching football.'

'I promised Jude he could see the end of the game.'

Two minutes were ticked out by the contracting pipes on the landing. With each click, my sinews tightened. I opened my eyes again to see shapes emerging from the blackness. The outline of my bathrobe hung from the cupboard door, like a ghostly figure, my mother, her shape tangible in the vague towelling outline, more sure a presence in the room than my own. Shadow and contrast visible, even in the dark, when I could not see anything of myself, could offer no proof that I was there. Bridget was still, but the breaths were not fluid enough for sleep. Awkwardly, over her shoulder, I cupped her breast.

Her voice came from a great distance. 'I'm tired.'

I sighed loudly and rolled back. 'It was the same last night.'

Another pause, silent and black.

'Let's try tomorrow, shall we?' Her voice was falling towards sleep.

'We've got dinner with Mike and Amy.'

'You invited them.'

'So, it's not your problem.' My words were normal speaking volume, but they rang like a shout in the dark.

'What's not my problem?'

I flipped over rapidly to face her again. The quilt twisted tight across my shoulders. 'Nothing's your problem.'

Bridget swivelled to face me. These revolutions of our bodies were futile; we couldn't see each other, but I sensed the gesture; it meant the fight was not conceded. We couldn't confront each other back to back.

'Don't do that, Tim.'

'I'm just trying to get you to talk about it.'

'It's been less than two weeks; you're overreacting.'

'It's driving me crazy.'

'*That* isn't my problem.'

'We have to talk.'

'Tomorrow. I can't think now.'

Once again she turned away, and then I did the same. I could hear the rhythm of her breath changing. Although the room was cooling, I was sweating. We lay, back to back, travelling away from each other. I tilted between rage and guilt for feeling angry. It was true, I let Jude stay up, deliberately exploited the Champions League semi-final: won some reprieve. Wasn't that doing her a favour? Lust was staved off while I sat in front of the television, the match providing ninety minutes of relative relaxation and then a surprise bonus: extra time, another fifteen minutes each way. She should have been cheering for a draw and penalties. Anything to stop my trigger-happy reaction that detonated the minute the final whistle blew.

I tugged the duvet higher over my shoulders. She couldn't just switch on her body and I couldn't switch mine off. I needed to seduce her properly and that took time we didn't have. Time I didn't have – without that connection it might happen again. This wasn't anything to do with Bridget. I gripped the pillow harder and tried to reach the safety of sleep.

I started to drift off but each time my mind touched on sex I lurched back from the brink of sleep. I worked at those thoughts, like a man trying to solve a puzzle. Since the children, the distance between us had grown. All the while she remained silent and her silence was most acrid when the room was dark; it caught in my throat like soot.

Then it happened again.

Thighs and shins prickle. Heat moves down the legs. Arms prickle, needle-points of fear. Clench fists. Pierce fingernails into palms. Hold onto darkness, the bed, the breathable air. Sheets, duvet. All dark, nothing to see in the dark. Starting to slip. Shoulders, neck, arms, slide into mattress. A jolt, falling, into the void. Nothing to fall, nobody. Only emptiness below the bed, a drift into emptiness. Cling to the shifting pillow, sink into darkness.

'Can you stop all that bloody noise?'

TWO

Jude's elbows rested on the breakfast bar with his face buried in the round between them, like a head on a massage table.

'Hey, Jude! How're you doing?'

He looked up sleepily. 'I'm fine' – he yawned – 'Can I have some breakfast?'

'Couldn't you find the cereal cupboard today?'

'But, Dad, I'm so tired.'

'I shouldn't have let you see the end of the match.'

'Da-a-a-d!' The word stretched into a whine. Then he lifted his face to see me holding a smile, waiting for him to notice. We both grinned.

We ate slowly, in a companionable quiet, apart from the munching sounds. We had a game to eat the cereal with our mouths open and make as much crunching as possible. Milk escaped in dribbles and a few splinters of cereal gathered on the breakfast bar. Jude tried not to laugh.

The autumn sunshine beamed through the skylight and my mood lifted. Each column of gold was ready to transport me. And the simple band around my finger seemed to shine brighter in the mornings. The immediate need had subsided the night before, as it always did. Today, my limbs were still clamped and uncomfortable, as if I were an alien in my own body, but even that was some reassurance. Visible arms and legs, tightness along the back, tiny twitches of skin and muscle, all vital signs to be monitored. The patient was alive and those other fears were distant now, the memory of a troubled dream.

Jude left his bowl on top of the dishwasher - a step in the right direction. Perhaps I could condition him like a lab rat to eventually put his dishes inside the washer; small rewards each time he approximated the desired behaviour. I said nothing; the boy was tired.

'I'm off to get dressed,' he said.

Our house was the largest of twenty that formed a *superior* development near Latchely village, each property individually drawn out by the architect, not one of those boxed-in modern estates. Our house stood equipped with everything from heated towel rails to closed-circuit television, to protect the family from external threats. The back garden swept away like a green sea, down to sycamores, giant gateposts to the Surrey countryside. We said Latchely was our dream, and that dream was still alive in the pools of sunlight that lay beneath each of the skylights.

Bridget was raking a brush violently through her long brown hair as she entered. 'You're still here,' she said, 'making coffee.'

'Making breakfast for Jude. Do you want one?'

'I'll have one later.'

'Anyway,' I said, reloading the coffee machine. 'What do you mean?'

'Nothing, you just seem to be working fairly random hours at the moment.'

'I was waiting to see Milo.'

'You hardly ever see him.'

She turned away briskly and started to unload the dishwasher, making enough clatter to chip the plates. The coffee machine pinged and I went to collect my cappuccino. I tried to decide if she intended her comment for me or Milo. Reproach always lurked in Bridget's voice, it was just a matter of working out if it was aimed at a specific target or part of a general bombardment against life. Milo seldom emerged before it was time to walk him to school.

'You could get him out of bed,' I said, and then regretted the dregs of resentment I could taste from last night.

'He's seven. He needs to start growing up a bit.'

'How's he supposed to know which bit?'

She stared at me, her face... and her eyes... and then resumed her assault on the crockery.

'Milo's old enough to dress himself,' she said.

'But you ration the television.'

'When I'm not undermined.'

I lifted my coffee to take a sip. When it came to feeding and bedtimes, she ruled the children strictly. If they caught colds or fevers, she pampered them and worried, keeping them back from school or hurtling to the doctor at the mildest symptom.

As she manoeuvred past, carrying a stack of plates, I swept the cup to the side, out of her path. A slop of coffee fell to the stone floor.

'Do you know how long it takes to clean that?' she said.

'It's okay, calm down, I'll wipe it.' I took a cloth from the cleaning cupboard.

'What are you saying, Tim, about Milo?'

'Just that the boys need a consistent message about what's expected.'

She gave a tiny shake of her head and went back to the dishwasher to collect the basket of cutlery. I sipped the coffee and tidied some bills into the brimming drawer, to give myself something to do, but I couldn't ignore the other presence in the room. We were the only two planets in space, orbiting each other but never colliding.

The floor was laid with stones that Sebastian called white slate. He'd withdrawn the heavy samples from a drawer in his dazzling showroom with a flourish that Bridget and I had found comical, and irresistible. I had no idea what the stone really was, some artificial material from a Scandinavian factory. The floor put another two thousand pounds on the house and delayed the completion by three weeks but we both thought it worth the wait and the cash. It was more than the dream we shared. It was a daily reminder, a trail of evidence. White stone. Proof that these visible arms, this mouth, this mind might leave a mark in the dirt. A house with slate floors, two cars, offices, children: all proof.

She held up the two soiled cereal bowls, retrieved from the clean dishwasher, one in each hand.

'It's not the end of the world.' I took them and rinsed them in the sink, then put the bowls back in the cupboard and finished my coffee.

White slate - the reward of a successful career, the place to succour a family. The stone's stratified lines reflected the spotlights under the kitchen units. All the houses in Latchely Gates came with *low voltage lighting installed throughout* - a phrase Sebastian recited so often he'd installed it in my memory. In the early days, in the first vacuum whiteness of the new kitchen, Bridget and I had promised each other we would fuck on that floor.

'Anyway, how can I be late for work?' I said.

I snatched my mobile from the granite surface and went to kiss Milo goodbye.

Memories of last night floated like unburstable bubbles, one of them being her promise to talk about it today. I knew that I could heave the subject into the open air myself, but this morning I lacked the will, as she had lacked it last night. I colluded with the silence. Partly it was pride, not to mention my problem in daylight. Partly I was childishly waiting for her to say something, something I knew she would never say. So, the scene would be repeated endlessly, like some forgotten show on a budget television channel.

Milo was not in his bed. I checked the nearest bathroom where he often sat for inexplicably long periods. Empty. From the top of the stairs, I shouted down to Bridget. She came to the bottom and glared up, cheeks drawn tight, shaking her head. Then we both called. We started to work through the house. As I came onto the landing from checking the en-suite bathroom, Bridget rushed forward shaking her hands like a ball-less juggler.

'Where the hell is he?' she said.

'Milo!' I yelled, as loud as I could, to match my level of hysteria to hers. Bridget flinched.

'What if he's run out of the house?' she said.

'I didn't hear the door. I don't think so.'

'You don't think. You don't think.'

'He can't be far. I'll go out.'

'No. Search the house again first.'

We revisited the other bedrooms, moving in a sort of united controlled panic. We opened cupboards, stuck our heads under beds and issued vague shouts. When I came back into the boys' bedroom, I noticed the open window, belted across the room and stuck my head out. Bridget came up beside me and we turned to each other. The relief drained through her face like fatigue.

Below me, protruding from the rear wall, was a porch roof that ran flat above the French windows. Beneath was a partly shaded patio where we sat in summer. When we bought the house I thought it an odd feature, not in keeping with the architecture. It wanted to be porticoed, with columns at the two corners, but it hung in the air, by magic. No signs of support showed, only the swathe of glass that flowed down to the patio. There was no room for brackets or corbels. When we moved in I wondered how long it would be before Milo attempted to clamber onto the roof; it was only five feet below the children's bedroom window and he was a fearless tree climber. I didn't know if it would shoulder the two boys' weight.

'Are you okay there?' I said.

Bridget's hip pressed against me as she squeezed in at the window.

'What the hell are you doing?' she said.

He looked up with a stubborn sulky face.

'Come on.' I leaned out of the window as far as I could, both arms extended.

'Milo, you could have killed yourself,' Bridget said.

He got to his feet slowly and reached out. I gripped under his shoulders and he clasped my elbows as if we were a trapeze act. Joined as one, it took all my strength to lift him. His feet slipped and scudded to gain a foothold on the wall. All the time, I couldn't help wondering if a nine-foot drop would actually destroy a seven-year-old.

'Be careful,' she said, as I hauled him up with his feet scrambling on the wall in a sort of reverse abseil. I lifted him over the window sill and planted him on his bed. Bridget and I sat either side. We both put our arms about his shoulders where they met below his blond curly hair.

'Are you okay?' I said.

'What's going on, Milo?' she asked and then leaned past his face to me and said, 'How many times have I asked you to put a lock on that window?'

'I'll do it,' I said. 'I've told the boys not to climb out.' Then I spoke to Milo again. 'What's the matter, my boy?'

'I came down,' he said, slowly. 'I heard you and mum arguing again.'

Isla Dunham

from Frogs in a Well

CHAPTER SEVEN

A PHOTOGRAPH OF THE PRESIDENT STARED OUT FROM AN ENORMOUS BILLBOARD outside the police headquarters. He was wearing white robes and his picture had been superimposed onto a Sri Lankan beach; he looked like a giant walking on water. Beneath the billboard, a checkpoint was manned by young soldiers in camouflage uniform with submachine guns slung casually over their shoulders. They waved Honor through. She walked past them purposefully, trying to disguise her nerves by giving the impression she knew exactly where she was going.

Nobody seemed to notice as she entered the dismal building. Two desk sergeants were shouting at an elderly woman whose head was bent over; she appeared to be weeping. Honor edged her way through a group of policemen in shiny white motorcycle helmets. They walked stiffly – like cowboys after a long ride – queuing up to store their guns in a coffin-shaped cupboard. A family of five sat on a long bench, staring hopelessly at the floor. A couple of officers with moustaches, their caps pulled down to their noses, were sharing a joke. There was something insane about the intensity of their laughter. Somewhere, a man was screaming.

'I could just walk back out,' she told herself. 'Nobody would notice. Shit, Bob Marley, I don't know if I can do this.'

She wished Mr Wellawatte was with her. She missed his paternal presence, his pedantic insistence on following due procedure, and felt irritated by his oblique excuses, his intimation that police stations were something respectable Sri Lankans just didn't do. Bob Marley had been more explicit. He'd told her in detail about the police's 'special' methods. The cigarette burns on the genitals, the whippings with rubber flex, the near suffocation with plastic bags soaked in petrol. Honor didn't feel equipped to face this reality. There was a terrifying difference between knowing something appalling was happening and actually having to see it.

Down a corridor she could see a row of dark cells with doors like metal cages. Was that where they were holding him? Was he being beaten up, chained to the floor like he said his friend had been? She tried to find the courage to look.

'What you want?' said a stern woman officer, hair scraped back in a bun, handcuffs and truncheon strapped to a heavy belt round her waist. 'This no place for tourists.'

'I have an appointment,' said Honor, her mind going blank. She fumbled in her bag for the piece of paper that Mr Wellawatte had given her. 'I am here to see DCI Pri...yan...tha Premika.'

It was like a shot had gone off.

'Why you not say?' the woman snapped. 'Come this way. Now.'

At a run, the woman took Honor down a long white-walled corridor. It led to a large wooden door guarded by two officers.

'Wait here,' said the woman, knocking on the door timidly before disappearing inside.

Honor could hear a powerful voice shouting on the other side of the door; a base so deep it sounded almost inhuman.

When she was eleven, she'd read an article in *The Observer* about torture and been physically sick. She'd insisted on joining Amnesty International and sat at the kitchen table writing letters to generals like Pinochet, Suharto and Ne Win, pleading with them to release prisoners of conscience whose names she could hardly spell. She had spent time over these letters, always using airmail paper and her fountain pen with blue ink, trying her best to think of what she could say that would persuade them to change their ways. She reasoned that everyone loved someone and these brutal dictators just needed to be reminded of this. *I know in your heart you are a kind man,* she would write. *I know you love your family. Please treat your prisoners as if they were your own father or your son.* It did not occur to her that they would not read her letters. Twenty years on, she had dropped her illusion about the fate of the letters, but she was still not ready to give up her faith in the hearts of the men who ignored them.

The door burst open. Fifteen officers trooped out looking cowed. Honor was ushered in; she reminded herself to breathe and to smile. Premika was seated behind a vast desk talking on one of the five phones lined in a row in front of him. He signalled to her to sit down.

The first thing that struck her was his sheer physical power. He had a vast barrel chest and broad shoulders and looked as if he could easily crush the phone in his massive hand. But there was also something polished about him. His skin was very smooth; his greying hair cut razor short; his uniform immaculate with shiny brass buttons and breast pockets groaning with neat rows of badges.

His office was panelled with wood and had the air of a corporate headquarters, rather than a provincial police station. There were two state-of-the-art computers and a fax machine. Air conditioners hummed in the background, an expensive lighting system compensated for the absence of windows. Glancing behind her, Honor saw a flat-screen television on the far wall showing live coverage of the cricket. Shelves lined the walls with photographs of Premika shaking hands with the president; Premika receiving large silver cups from distinguished men in elaborate uniforms; Premika at the head of a legion of officers; Premika playing polo; and Premika at the snowy summit of a mountain.

'Forgive me for that rumpus earlier,' he said, putting down the phone. He spoke softly with only a slight Sri Lankan accent. 'A minor disciplinary matter. This is a new posting for me. This place is a mess. Some of the men are complete idiots. I was telling them they are meant to be my eyes and ears, not blunt instruments.'

He smiled. Now she could see a softness to his face and something unnervingly sympathetic about his large brown eyes. He pressed a red button on his desk and an officer appeared instantly at the door.

'Would you like tea or something stronger?'

'Tea, please,' said Honor, her voice sounding much higher than she expected.

'Where are you from?' he asked.

'London,' she said, forcing a smile.

'I was in Newcastle last year,' he said. 'Do you know the Sandersons? Mike and Angela. He teaches physics at the university. He's an expert on sub-microscopic particle research. '

Honor apologised. She did not know the Sandersons and had never been to Newcastle.

'Beautiful city. Many fine bridges. Marvellous cheesecake. But too cold. Even in April.'

She tried to imagine Premika shivering in a tea-shop wearing an anorak.

He turned to his computer keyboard and tapped a few keys. 'I see from my notes that Somarathne Wellawatte made an appointment for you about an incident at the train station at approximately 11.48 this morning. What were you doing at the station? It is not exactly a beauty spot.'

Honor told him about how she wanted to help the children who begged there; the baby left naked lying under newspaper, sleeping in a pool of its own urine; the girls living by the rubbish dump with open sores all over their legs. She described how the children were trapped in a hopeless world of exploitation and neglect and, to her surprise, found that he was actually listening and looked genuinely upset.

'Terrible, just terrible,' he said. 'I go out at six every morning on my bicycle in shorts and a vest, nobody recognises me, and it's the only way I get to know what's really going on. I, too, am very worried about these children. It is important work that you are doing.'

Was it her anxiety or was it just the pure relief of talking to someone who understood that made Honor say much more than she intended? She had not realised how angry she was with Upali. Until then, all her thoughts had been focused on her fear of him and her feelings of powerlessness.

'He is truly evil,' she said. 'He forces the children to beg, makes girls as young as five carry screaming babies. He takes whatever they get. He whips them with a metal chain to control them. I have seen the scars on their skin. Some of those kids are so beautiful and there is so much prostitution. I can't believe he is not involved.'

'And he hit you?' Premika said, still listening intently.

'I am sure he would have," she said. "He said he would rape me if I did not leave the children alone.'

'Do you have witnesses?' Premika asked gently.

'He whispered it," she said. 'His mouth was pressed into my ear. It was disgusting.'

'Such people are worse than cancer,' he said, suddenly angry. 'I know this Upali. We are holding him here. It was so much easier in the days when we could just bump people off. Two officers on motorbikes, a bullet in the early morning. It was all sorted out efficiently.'

He pushed back his chair and rubbed his eyes. He looked suddenly tired. She noticed that the knuckles on his right hand were slightly discoloured as if bruised. Surely it was her imagination. Red lights were flashing on four of the telephones in front of him in silent anger, calling for his attention.

'These days, I have all the human rights people breathing down my neck. It makes my job so much more difficult.' He picked up one of the phones and barked some instructions into the receiver. He was speaking so forcefully it was hard to understand the rapid mixture of English and Sinhala. But then she caught one word: 'Vanish.' He repeated it again - and then for a third time.

For a moment Honor was taken back to a sunlit classroom and her history teacher, Mr Aston. She was fourteen and they were studying the American Civil Rights Movement. He read from a speech by Martin Luther King and she remembered being so inspired by one phrase that she wrote it out on the front of all her school books. *We have to repent in this generation nor so much for the evil deeds of the wicked people but for the appalling silence of the good.* At fourteen, she had vowed never to be silent. But now, these words were like a knife to her throat.

'Don't worry,' he said with a smile. 'It is all taken care of. That man will never bother you again.'

A police officer brought in a tea tray. The china was porcelain and decorated with flowers, the teaspoons – silver. Honor's hands were shaking, her mind frozen with shock.

'Just milk, please,' she said, and hoped he didn't notice the cup rattling on its saucer as she took it from him. Surely she should say something. Persuade Premika to be lenient and to feel the same compassion he would feel if Upali was his own son. And yet, she said nothing.

'Yes!' Premika punched the air with his fist. 'Malinga's just bowled England's captain with a great inswinger. We've got them in trouble at 97 for 4.' He reached for an ornate box on his desk which was carved in the teardrop shape of Sri Lanka and had the President's grinning face engraved on it. He took out his name card and wrote his mobile phone number on the back with a Montblanc pen. 'Is there anything else?' he asked.

'The man who stopped Upali hitting me. I think you are also holding him. His name is Bob Marley.'

'I am sure we have him along with Mick Jagger and Elvis Presley.'

'He has long hair and was badly beaten up.'

'That could be a number of people.'

'He is...' She tired to think of a way of identifying him, tongue-tied by guilt that she didn't even know his real name. 'He is... kind,' she said, feeling stupid.

'Oh, that will make him easy to identify,' Premika said with a staccato burst of laughter. 'I will see what I can do.' He stood up, signalling the meeting was over. 'Call me anytime. Night or day.' And he shook her hand – holding it for several seconds longer than was comfortable.

Rosie Rowell

Telling Stories

MY DAD BELIEVED IN STORIES. STORIES WERE HIS LITURGY, HIS CREED, HIS affirmation of life. He believed stories held in them the spirit of the ancients. He believed they wove threads around us that held us together, that made us belong. My mother believed my father was soft in the head. Her world rotated on an axis of reason and logic. Anything that could not be substantiated by fact was dismissed. Fate and soul-mates and intuition were the stuff of bad novels. So she stayed stuck forever on the precipice, the non-believer, looking out on my father's world, a world both large enough to span universes and eons of time, and as small and fragile as raindrops caught in a spider's web, too scared to ever take that tiny leap and ask, 'But what if?'

Her crippling inability to get past the rational made her the very worst reader of stories. One of my earliest memories was of her breaking off midway through the story of Noah's Ark to inform me that there was obviously no way Noah could fit all the animals in the world on his boat.

'So the rest of them drowned?' I asked in a horrified whisper.

'No, no,' she said with a little laugh. 'We're not supposed to take it literally. We're not supposed to believe it. The story is a metaphor.' A few seconds passed as mother and daughter stared hopelessly at each other. 'It's not really about a boat, or animals.'

'What's it about?' I asked, entirely baffled.

'Sin,' she replied, 'and disobedience.'

That was, by mutual agreement, the last story she ever read.

So it was my dad who read to us at night, Beth and I tucked under an arm each, the three of us cocooned in the mosquito net that hung over my bed. My father's voice rose and fell as he brought Julian and Anne and George to life as they set foot on their island for the first time; or the cheeky Pippi Longstocking, which he insisted on reading in Afrikaans, because it sounded funnier; the winsome Anne of Green Gables; or daring and sassy Nancy Drew.

But the best stories came out on our compulsory 'family fun days' – when, by the time the sun was properly up, we'd already be halfway over the steep pass that took us deep into the belly of the mountains. Under a crisp, blue sky we'd leave our dust-sprayed station wagon where the dirt road stopped and, armed with sandwiches and bottles of Oros and sun hats, we'd make for the caves a few hours away, zig-zagging up the narrow footpaths – my dad at the front, Beth, me and often Simon at the back. Just like a group of San hunters setting off.

As he marched ahead, waving his walking stick in front of him to ward off sleepy cobras, my father conjured up his favourite characters, as real as if they were walking in front of us. We became the hunters, our sights set on an eland or an elephant, vigilantly following even the faintest track until perhaps after a day or so we found fresh dung. And in our excitement we grew as quiet as breath, as invisible as a breeze, as light as dew, as we gained ground on the unsuspecting herd.

In the heat of the day we retreated, hot and thirsty and hungry, to the cool of a rocky outcrop, a good vantage point on the valleys below. Whilst rusty-brown figures chased elephants with brandished arrows on the smooth rock face behind us, we became the waiting women-folk.

The hunting party had been gone a number of days by now. As we tucked into our cheese and tomato sandwiches, we scrunched up our eyes anxiously for a scuffle or a dust cloud, for a sign that all was well.

Later, retracing our steps on wary knees from a long day's walk, we'd hear about the happy reunion, about the hunters returning home, bursting with stories of bravery and skill. We'd hold our breath as my dad recounted their final breathtaking moments of the chase and stop dead as the poisoned arrow pierced the heart of the unlucky eland. Here my dad would pause, and we'd remind him that a hunter would always apologize to the fallen eland, and pay homage to the great beast. And then with a smile, he'd launch into the dancing and feasting that followed a successful hunt and the ancient spirits who visited upon them in the deep of the night.

As if on cue, as if beckoned back from the spirit world, I turned away from the dark garden to see Beth. She was standing just behind me, gazing towards the ascending moon, barefoot and in her white nightie, illuminated from behind by the pool of light that shone out from the open door.

'It's a bushman moon,' she said, and smiled.

And then, scattering the mournful spirits, she yelled: 'Dad! Dad! Come tell us a story. It's a story-telling moon.'

My dad and mum appeared at the door.

'But it's late,' murmured my mother. 'Why are you both –'

'Nonsense,' said my dad mildly. 'It's the perfect time for a story.'

We settled ourselves outside on the *stoep* on the wide cushioned *riempie* bench: my mum, Beth, me and my dad on the end, and for a moment even the cicadas and the frogs seemed to hush in anticipation.

'Which one do you want?' asked my dad, his low voice hummed in tune with the night.

'The story of Leopold,' said Beth firmly, 'The story of how it all began.'

'Really?' asked my mum. 'Do we really want that one again?'

'Yes,' replied Beth. 'Begin!'

We sat in a row, warming each other against the cool August night. We were a set, the four of us: at a cellular level, we matched. But sometimes I worried that this wasn't enough. What else would hold us together? I didn't feel a deep sense of belonging to my family, or even similar to any of them. In fact, most days, basic communication was difficult enough.

My mother leaned forward, as if reading my thoughts, and smiled at me. I scowled and shifted slightly so that I couldn't see her anymore.

'In the beginning,' began my dad, 'in the very beginning was darkness and a heartbeat, the heartbeat of infinite time. And in the midst of this, a young planet moving, growing, breaking apart. Breathing in time to the ancient heartbeat, the heartbeat that will survive long after we've killed ourselves off. We're all just visitors, you know, a plague of fleas on a dog's back.'

'All right,' I said. 'Moving on.' We were in grave danger of being swallowed up by tectonic plates and continental shelves. 'And then came the animals,' I prompted.

'And then came the animals,' agreed my dad. 'Of course, that is just fascinating, the story of how the animals came to be, how life formed out of matter –'

No,' said Beth firmly. 'Not tonight.'

'A son would have been interested,' he said forlornly.

'Tough *takkies*,' replied Beth.

'Well, then, if you're happy to skip a few eons, then came the "early race". Animals were people and people animals and they lived side by side and the animals knew as much as people and everyone knew to revere the *kaggen*. Because he was clever and more powerful than any of the other animals. He was the supreme hunter...'

'*Ja, ja*, we know about the *kaggen*,' said Beth quickly, because my dad would happily slip into bushmen stories about the praying mantis and forget the Leopold story altogether.

He smiled at her and said, 'Okay – after the early race came the modern race, where people became more powerful than animals and people hunted animals. And then the white man discovered the tip of Africa, and brought about the age when people hunted people. So where are we now? 1803. Johannes Basson Leopold, and his wife Helena and seven children were recently arrived in the Cape, looking for a new life and fortune. But it was hard there in the Cape; it wasn't anything like they'd been promised back in Holland. Everyone was talking about an empty Eden just waiting for them up north, beyond the Hex River Mountains, beyond the endless rules of the small colony. So one day Johannes said to his wife, "*Poplap*, I'm sick to death of these bladdy Brits, with all their rules."' My dad paused to allow us a giggle and shoot a glance at my mother. "'Let's go north," Johannes said to his anxious Helena, "We'll keep going until we find a beautiful valley, lush and green and far away from the Cape." So he hitched up his wagons, loaded up his seven children and a handful of slaves and off they went.'

'Do you think they started off in a big group? Along with many other families?' asked Beth, who needed the story to be the same each time.

My dad scratched his chin. 'I think they did. But our Leopold was a difficult fellow, an argumentative type.' He leaned over and patted my mother's knee playfully.

Beth laughed in delight.

'So it wasn't long before he broke away from the big group who were headed up north towards vast open plains and gold and diamonds. And instead, Leopold turned his wagons and his few head of cattle east. And they got as far as this valley, just as far as here,' my dad stamped his foot, 'and stopped.'

After a pause I looked up into three expectant faces. 'What?' I said.

'Come on,' prompted Beth.

I sighed and rolled my eyes, then dutifully delivered what was historically my line: 'But why? Why would they stop here? I mean, there's nothing here.'

'I don't know,' replied my father in all seriousness. 'Maybe there was sickness in the family, or maybe Leopold looked at the mountains looming up ahead and realised they'd never make it across. But then again they'd come too far to turn back, so here they stayed.' He stroked the back of my hair. 'Or maybe Helena climbed down from her wagon one day and marched up to her husband and said: "Dammit, Johannes, my mother was right about you. I've had it with this wagon and I've had it with this endless search: just over the next hill, the next valley. So far and no further." And that was that. So Leopold built a house, this house. And they must have sat here, too, looking out on the heavy moon, listening to the night sounds, telling stories.'

And in a moment I could almost swear I heard the Leopold children just beyond the shadows.

'A few hard years down the line more farmers trickled into the valley,' continued my dad. 'And of course the bladdy English with their rules caught up with them eventually. But they didn't stay long.' My dad winked at my mum.

'Well, we're back!' said my mum, standing up, 'with our bloody rules. And now to bed. All of you.'

As she lifted my head with both hands to kiss me good night, the spell was broken and my body froze at her closeness.

'Promise me you'll not cause any more trouble,' I said severely.

My mother's lips were smiling as she kissed my cheek. 'I promise,' she said. 'From now on, I shall be as good as gold.'

I used to believe in my dad's stories without question, until one day he told me that each one of us is born with a story. When I asked him to tell me my story, he refused outright; he said it was mine to live. But when I nagged him within an inch of his life, he said I had a nomad's spirit, that deep inside I carried the song of the ancients, I was one of them. That was when I decided that perhaps my mum was right, perhaps really he was a little bit soft in the head after all.

Sarah Sotheron

Breeding

IT WAS JUNE 1940. SMART STUMBLED INTO THE STUDY WITHOUT KNOCKING. HE was breathless and still in the apron he wore when cleaning silver, heavily smeared with streaks of pink paste and dark patches of tarnish. As he hurried towards me, he became aware of it and struggled to bunch it up, trying to push it round behind him out of sight with one hand. In the other, he held a silver salver on which rested a piece of paper.

'Telegram, Madam,' he said, his voice seeming deeper than usual.

I picked it up. 'Thank you,' I said.

He hesitated for a moment or two then turned and left the room.

In the eight months since Philip had left for the war I'd had only a few brief airmail letters and a birthday phone call on a line so bad that we'd had to give up. The telegram said he was Missing in Action. I called Willoughby straight away and we arranged to meet that night for dinner.

'How often does "Missing in Action" mean dead?' I asked.

I could tell in the pause that followed that he was weighing up how truthful to be. 'Probably half the time,' he said. His hand was holding mine across the table and he squeezed it a little more tightly.

'It's rather more than half the time, isn't it?' I asked.

'Perhaps,' he said reluctantly.

I tried to think what Philip being dead would mean. The worldly aspects of my present life were all entirely due to him – hadn't even existed two years ago: the house in which I lived, the bed in which I slept, the food I ate, the money I spent, the clothes I wore, the servants he'd chosen, even my lover was due to his introduction. Without him what would be left? Would I revert to being the child I'd been before we married? There'd still be Willoughby, though. Wouldn't there? My cashmere cardigan seemed suddenly scratchy and I took it off, pulling my hand from his. If Philip were dead would Willoughby's wife view me differently and see me as a threat, a predatory single woman?

'Do you think Patricia suspects?' I asked him.

'No,' he said.

'Would she bring it up if she did?'

'No idea,' said Willoughby.

'Does it worry you?'

'Not in the least.'

'Would she leave you if she knew?'

'Maybe,' he said.

'Maybe,' I said, 'she's got a lover herself.' I wanted to ruffle his irritatingly calm demeanour.

Willoughby smiled. 'Can't see it.'

'You're so cocky.'

'No need for her to take a lover,' said Willoughby. 'Why would she?'

'Unbearably cocky.'

'I think she finds her marital obligations more than sufficient.'

'It's not always about bed,' I said.

'Even so.'

My heart began to quicken. 'Do you still make love then?' I asked. It hadn't really occurred to me. Willoughby had inferred Patricia wasn't keen on that side of marriage and now he had me so why would they?

'Rarely,' he said, a little carefully for my liking.

Little needles were dancing in and out of my internal organs, the ones under my ribs.

'When was the last time?'

He glanced at me. 'Probably,' he hesitated, and the needles upped their rhythm, 'her birthday?' I didn't like his lack of sureness.

'When was it?' I asked.

'When was what?' he said.

'Her birthday.'

'Nineteenth of March.' I felt my face wince, although I was struggling to control it.

'Surely if she's so disinterested in sex, it wouldn't be the best birthday present for her.' I tried to keep my voice light but the words sounded as sour as they tasted.

Willoughby said nothing, his expression remaining relaxed.

'I only make love to you.' I could hear that my voice was whining. 'I've been faithful.'

Willoughby snorted and his face broke into one of those infuriating foxy grins. 'Faithful,' he said with irony.

'Don't.' My voice was a shout. 'Philip might be dead. He's been away eight months. I might not have been unfaithful, not for...' I struggled with how to continue, 'weeks... or however long he's been dead for.' And then I started to cry and Willoughby moved across to comfort me. Whether or not what that comfort turned into was, at that moment, an act of adultery, I had no idea, and somehow it ceased to be important very quickly.

The first white postcard arrived in the second post, on a Friday at the beginning of September. It was one of those hot, airless days when the atmosphere feels like a vacuum that's trying to suck all life from you. In every room there seemed to be trapped flies buzzing fruitlessly against the windows. The postcard had black strips taped across some of the words which were written in pencil in Philip's spidery hand. Some of the writing had almost rubbed away.

'Darling E, I'm a POW in – *a stretch of black tape followed.* We're allowed to send a p.c. of 60 words each month. Please send – *more black tape.* I broke my leg during – *more tape* - but it's mending well, slow though. Food no worse than school. Good set of men. *A long stretch of tape.* How are you? And all at home? Pls send news. Missing you terribly, Your loving Philip.'

The next day I received an official letter from the War Office stating that Philip was a prisoner of war in Oflag 17 and that any mail or parcels should be sent via the Red Cross.

The grandmother clock in the hall struck five. It must be later than that, surely. I couldn't ask Smart to get me a drink quite this early. Even when I asked at six it often seemed to take an age. Sometimes I suspected a deliberate delay. Luckily I'd taken to keeping an extra supply of gin in a cabinet in the drawing room so as not to always have to bother him. With the extra hours he now had to find for Home Watch it surely made sense to cut down his duties where I could. When I opened the cupboard, I couldn't see the bottle at first, but then I remembered I'd hidden it behind our snakeskin backgammon board. It was just that I didn't want to tempt the servants.

Willoughby took me out to celebrate the news that Philip was safe.

We were holding hands again, both seated on red velvet banquettes at La Taverna, one of increasingly few restaurants to remain open. Willoughby was in ebullient mood, looking intently into my eyes, but then dropping his gaze to my cleavage where it lingered before returning to my face. It was as if he was touching me, his brazen admiration communicating directly with my skin, and despite the increasingly rare treat of fresh fish I pushed the lemon sole around my plate, my hunger having metamorphosed into desire. I wanted to leave the restaurant, be somewhere private.

'I've got a bit of news,' he said.

I was looking at his eyebrows. That evening they seemed wild, almost unkempt, somehow promising unbridled potency. I wanted to run my fingers along them, try to tame them, though knowing I'd fail.

'Good or bad?' I asked.

'Depends on how you look at it,' he said. Something in his tone rattled me.

'How will I look at it?' I asked

'Sensibly, I hope,' he said. 'Pragmatically.'

'You're being sent away again,' I said. It was my worst fear.

'No,' he said.

'Well, what?'

'Patricia's pregnant.'

I stared at him. 'But how can she be?'

He gave a wry smile.

'But she isn't the maternal type.'

'She seems very happy with the news.'

'What if I were pregnant, too?'

Willoughby looked at me strangely. 'But you're not,' he said.

'What if I was?'

'We'd have some difficult decisions,' he said.

'You'd expect me to get rid of it,' I said, suddenly knowing that I couldn't ever do that with Willoughby's child.

'You're not pregnant,' he said 'Patricia's pregnant.'

'I want a baby,' I said, but what I really wanted at that moment was all of Willoughby, his whole focus, not to have to share his attention with others, with a wife, for all the 'news' in his life to be about me. 'A new baby will mean I see even less of you. When's it due?'

'Not necessarily,' he said. 'It's due in February.'

I felt icy cold. I glanced at my upper arms. Goosebumps had appeared on the skin. 'So it's not just birthdays.'

He didn't seem to understand, staring at me quizzically.

'You said you only fucked her on her birthday,' I spat, standing up, pushing the table towards him so that glasses wobbled and cutlery rattled. 'I'm going home.' I turned and walked to the entrance, asking the maître d' to get my coat. Willoughby had pushed back his chair and risen slightly when I stood, but had made no attempt to stop me.

'Bastard,' I thought.

I took a cab back to the flat, soothed myself with a tiny nip of brandy and fell into a petulant sleep.

I was woken by sirens. Airfields and military positions around London had been attacked in the previous weeks and there were fears that some navigational error might mean stray bombs hitting the capital. I was too tired to gather my things and go to the shelter. At that moment, my life seemed far from precious. If anything happened it would be Willoughby's fault.

By the morning I had accepted Patricia's pregnancy. Perhaps there was a silver lining. Surely it was likely that as her body became huge and distorted, those 'rare' occasions would cease altogether. He would desire me more than ever.

It was May 1945. The war was grinding to a halt. I hadn't seen Philip for five years and eight months. We had not even shared one-sixth of that time as man and wife before he left. German defeat was anticipated any day now and it seemed I was one of the few people in the country who felt some ambivalence. I knew what it meant. I had known since I boarded the train to London to meet Willoughby that first time. The relationship must end with the war. That had been my justification. Morals could be suspended in wartime whilst all our lives hung by a thread. I'd been abandoned within months of my marriage. No wonder I'd accepted comfort. Circumstances had been extreme. Now there was to be a last supper.

Smart had killed one of the chickens – it hadn't been laying well – and Mrs Hitchins made a pie. She looked horrified when I said that I'd be taking it to London. 'Surely you won't need the whole thing, Madam?'

Two precious eggs were used to make a chocolate mousse. Willoughby loved puddings and I used some of the black-market rations previously destined for Philip as it seemed there would be no need to make up any more Red Cross parcels. I even added a pre-war tin of cashew nuts to the stash and picked some spring flowers from the garden.

An officer from Windsor gave me a lift to London – the trains were so infrequent. It was a broken city we drove through, huge swathes of buildings reduced to rubble. Walking even the shortest distance was hazardous, avoiding piles of debris and all the many dangerous buildings awaiting demolition with their precarious temporary props which often failed. Although Park Mansions was unscathed, bombs had fallen all around – in Basil Street, in

Lowndes Square, even Raphael Street, just behind us, that connected Knightsbridge Green to Trevor Square.

Willoughby arrived in uniform, smiling broadly. He pointed to the epaulette on his shoulder. 'General,' he announced. 'Found out today. See the crossed swords?'

I looked at the little gold markings, trying to remember how they'd been before and seeing little difference. 'Darling,' I said. 'How amazing. A General.' The word moved pleasurably around inside my mouth. It tasted better than Brigadier. Willoughby was recognised as an important, successful man and he desired me.

He was picking at the cashew nuts. 'Clever girl,' he said. 'Finding them.' He came over and kissed me. 'Shall we have a different sort of hors d'oeuvre now?' he said.

'The pie will overcook,' I said. 'It's nearly ready.'

Willoughby walked to the kitchen and turned off the oven. 'Cold pie later,' he said, but it was several hours before we lay in the bed, empty plates finally on the floor beside us.

I moved into the crook of his arm as he smoked a cigarette, giving me occasional puffs. I loved these moments.

'It'll be over within days,' he said.

'You know what that means,' I said. My stomach gave a little spasm, like an oyster squeezed with lemon.

He looked at me, one of those eyebrows I so loved raising itself a tiny bit.

'This must end, too,' I said

'If you think that's best.' His voice was entirely neutral.

'I can't go on once Philip comes home.'

'So,' he said. 'No more.' And he leant across to kiss the nearest nipple which immediately stiffened in response.

'Perhaps one more meeting.' The words came out despite myself.

'I've got to go to Catterick. Tomorrow, I think. Training. Be there two or three weeks, I imagine.'

'Well, this is probably it then,' I said.

Willoughby leaned over me again, staring down. I wanted to reach up, encircle him and pull him down onto me. 'So, it's over.'

'It has to be,' I said, my insides clenching, squeezing the pie I had just eaten back towards my throat.

He reached down to the bottle of wine on the floor, then across me to fill my glass before doing the same with his. 'It's been quite a ride,' he said.

David S. Hickson

A Mass Murderer in Heaven

CHAPTER ONE

Kettleness: half-a-hamlet, harbourer of a mass murderer.

SOME FIVE HOURS AND TWO CHANGES SINCE IT LEFT KING'S CROSS, THE 6.15 chugged into Whitby. Outside the station I crunched towards a taxi driver wearing an unzipped parka coat and, angled on his head, a New York Giants baseball cap now faded to slate. He watched my every step without expression.

Instead of immediately responding when I asked him to take me to Miss Jules' B&B, Kettleness he held the lip of the cap between mouldy thumb and forefinger and slid it into a second angle. I rocked in the wind.

After a moment he nodded. 'Best get in then, I reckon,' he said.

It wasn't long before we were out of Whitby heading north up the coast road. I was warm in the cab, but the wind thumped at its window. The twitching North Sea pretended not to notice.

'Ugly as buggery, n'tit.'

'Hmm,' I replied, unsure what he was talking about.

'Caused by quarrying alum.' He tapped the driver side window with a sovereign ring. 'S'why ruddy cliffs look like ruddy buggery,' he said.

After a moment's focus I saw them. Misshapen dune-sized lumps, moon-grey at root but suffering an acne of green and pink seaside brush, disfigured the cliffs' profile. 'Odd,' I said.

'Alum tombstones,' he said. I caught his hooded eye in the rear-view mirror. 'Back in olden days they mined the alum shale, piled t'up, ruddy scorched it for its oil then... guess what? Any idea what they'd add t'alum t'make ruddy leather soft?' I didn't have a clue what alum was, never mind what they added to it to soften leather, so I shrugged my shoulders. The car slowed. The taxi driver bent his head around his seat, breathing nicotine. 'Ruddy piss,' he said.

A few minutes or so later, he pointed to a small hamlet of six or seven red-brick buildings cowering before the sea. 'That there's Kettleness - on yonder headland. Farthest point of the coast.' The cab bumped over a rock, my forehead knocked against the window while I strained to make out Kettleness.

'Is that all of it?'

'Oh, no,' he said. Once again I caught his hooded eye in the rear-view mirror. 'Only half of it,' he said.

'Ah, right,' I said, settling back into my seat.

'T'other half fell int'ruddy sea 'bout hundred an' fifty year ago.'

Arriving at Miss Jules' B&B, I pushed hard a worn-smooth brass doorbell with a cold thumb. It shrieked.

The door opened, Miss Jules' thin eyes appeared, adjusted themselves on their perch, and asked me if I was black.

Perhaps it was the approaching evening that darkened my hair as it was usually blonde – the colour of masking tape. I asked her if it mattered.

'Nancy-boy, then?' she said.

I turned my head. The November North Sea wind played whore with my teeth – brushing up close but cold. Should I stroll off? Take a stand? But where else could I stay for the month or so I'd be holed up in the arse-end of obscurity?

'In which case,' she continued, 'you must be Number 2.' She opened the door wider.

The smell of washing drying made my eyes ache. My treacherous feet found a brown doormat just inside. I scuffed my trainers clean of the journey and relieved my back of the rucksack's weight.

'Just so long as you're not French, mind.' She clumped up a buckling red stair carpet in charcoal boots, shouting: 'Come far?'

'London.'

'Southerners,' she said, and tutted.

Upstairs, a fool's gold number 2 was glued to an off-cream door. Miss Jules drew a key from a holster. Bent, she bumped the key into the key-hole. 'You're in here,' she said to the door. She turned to me. 'Bingo. Full house.' Broken-egg eyes not moving from mine, she slowly clicked open the latch. The door gave way. 'Couple upstairs in 3,' she hung on the door handle, 'Hewson and Jablonski. Not married, mind.' She sniffed. With a prod of her nose she indicated over my left shoulder. I turned. 'And in there' – her voice was pallid in my ear – 'Mr Churchill.' The door to Number 1 skulked in its dark blanket. I turned back, but Miss Jules lingered on Number 1. With the crook of a first finger she brushed up the spectral hair on her upper lip; the knee of her middle finger blotted cardinal lipstick. I put her age in the early fifties, then thought myself too kind by half.

She leaned against my door and fell in. On entering, we startled the dust drifting in the late afternoon half light. I had to duck under a close ceiling which for me is an alien reflex. Emulsion clogged the gaps between the cobbles on the walls. The window's teeth chattered in the wind while behind it the North Sea heaved.

A single bed hunched in a corner. Miss Jules watched me via an oval mirror on an avocado dressing table.

'Very nice,' I said to her reflection.

'Breakfast in the kitchen between seven and eight. No later, mind. A month, you say?' I had said, on the phone, a fortnight, when I reserved the room. 'What business around here takes a month?'

I brushed past her and winded the bed by landing the rucksack onto its solar plexus. I sat on its head. I folded my legs. Miss Jules smoothed down the dressing table's side.

'I've got a temporary job.'

She looked up at me. 'Oh.'

'With Professor Vingel.' I investigated the possibility of a smile.

She sniffed again, turned, found the door handle, opened the door and was part-way gone. 'I was right,' she said. Not turning round. 'You *are* black.'

The door rattled shut.

I disembowelled the rucksack, first filling a grumbling ward-robe, then the drawers under the avocado dressing table. After an hour or so I decided to head to the sea. I opened my door. A syn-copated beat later, the door to Number 1 opened. A man appeared in the shadow.

'Hi,' he called. The man stretched forward at pace. A pinch pot face emerged from an ill-matched suit. Its jacket sagged on a chicken-wire frame. He wore emaciated trainers. 'Ah, Mr Johnson. Just arrived?' Tinge of Essex or Kent.

'3.15 into Whitby.'

'Winston Churchill,' he said, holding out a daddy-long-legs hand. 'Not the original.' My stomach sighed. How many times had he felt the need to say that? His other hand told me to Fuck Off with a V-sign. My heart clenched a fist before realising it was a Churchillian victory, and released. I was about to offer my name but, too long after I should have been alerted to its curiosity, I reg-istered that he already knew it. Instead, I shook his non-abusive hand with a quick slap. He clung on. 'Need a guide to see the sights? I've been around here a good *demi*-year.'

'Hmm.'

'I see myself as a sort of missionary,' he said, nostrils twitching.

I headed for the stairs. He kept up with a skip.

'I'm just going to check out the sea,' I said. 'I understand it's dramatic at this time of year.'

'In a breeze like this it'll be nothing short of exhilarating; I'll show you the way!'

'S'okay. I imagine it's pretty difficult to miss.'

'That it is, ha ha! Big old blue thing. Due East. Will be wet!'

I'd reached the bottom of the stairs and used the straight to put distance between us. I was at the front door by the time he'd clat-tered down.

'Catch up later, then?'

I offered him no more than a non-committal jerk of the chin.

'Watch out for the dinosaurs!' he called.

Tree Garnett

Poker

CHAPTER FIVE
14 July 1983

"You must never count your money when you're sitting at the table."

Poker. Daisy knew the other twelve-year-olds at school did not play poker, bridge or blackjack with their parents. They did not know if you should twist or stick when you had a 10 and 6. They did not know the dreamt-of glory that was a royal straight flush. Daisy knew, too, that Sam had to be the only six-year-old well versed in bluffing and the ins and outs of five-card stud high-low. But this was their routine each time they came to stay with their father. It always had been, as long as she could remember. They would not stare at penguins in the zoo, and they would not fly their kites on Hampstead Heath. Just this. Just gambling and bluffing and raising and hoping for a full house or threes at the the very least. Now she was tired, though, tired from Tad's cease-less wisdoms on when to raise or fold, or how not to get shot at the poker table.

Sam's eyes were small and round as marbles, and as he yawned, his head drooped forwards. They had played hand after hand since lunchtime and the ashtray next to Tad was piled with crumpled cigarette butts. A thin layer of smoke hung above them like a cloud. Across the road in the communal gardens she could see families ending their day. Mothers were gathering up their picnic rugs and pulling toddlers from the sandpit. From here, their move-

ments, the bending and standing and bending down again, reminded Daisy of a casual but ancient dance. She saw the mothers
waving goodbye to friends and departing the gardens, clanking
the metal gate behind them. The leaves had just begun to shift
and jostle in the green canopy above the square and Daisy tried
to imagine the beginnings of an evening breeze, how it might feel
to be walking home after a day outdoors, like being on holiday
in France when the cooling air made contact with your sunburnt
skin. There was a moment in summer when it seemed possible
that it would always be this way, when she forgot that the leaves
would soon turn copper and that the light would dwindle.

It was her turn to deal, but she did not pick up the pack of
cards. 'Dad, I'm really hungry. Can we stop now?'

Tad looked at his watch, 'Five fifteen, we've only just begun. I
need to win my money back. But okay,' He winked at Cindy, 'Shall
we call it six?' Then, turning formally to Sam and Daisy, he announced, 'You know this lady here makes one mean cocktail,' and
he winked again.

Sam looked at Daisy across the sprawl of chips on the green
baize and he winked too and she laughed, then spluttered, pieces
of popcorn spraying across the mess of cards and glasses.

'Okay, guys, this is a cocktail pause. Who needs to pee?' Tad
shimmied across the carpet, heading for the drinks; his boots were
still on and he stamped three times, like a cowboy or a Latin dancer.

'Can I do the ice?' Sam had opened an ice bucket covered with
black crocodile skin and was jabbing the tongs into the solid mass
inside.

Tad's home was a million miles different from their mother's
house. Here there was a lacquered green drinks cabinet that opened
to reveal ranks of backlit glasses and bottles posing in spotlights.
These were tall and squat, familiar and foreign. Daisy recognised
the whisky, of course, the blue bottle of gin, the vodka and the
Angostura Bitters. At home there was no cocktail shaker, no well-
thumbed book with instructions for White Ladies and Manhattans,
for half measures, sugar syrup, grenadine and lime.

'Do you know how to juggle, Sam?' Cindy had four lemons

and deftly threw them into the air where they rotated and changed places again, again, again.

'Let me have a go.' Daisy caught a lemon that Cindy threw to her and she took turns with Sam as they tried to copy her impossible coordination.

'Who's forgotten their jobs?' Tad was back in the room with a tray of food. 'I'll have a Scotch on the rocks – measure out three fingers please Sam – and Cindy here likes vodka with tonic, don't you, Baby? Daisy, here, help me put this out.'

Their meal was sweet corn, rice and chicken plastered with a layer of yellow breadcrumbs. Daisy set down a plate beside each player's place. The food at Tad's house was either got from Harrods Food Hall or, more often now, was born inside the microwave. Those were miraculous meals that came to life after merely minutes of revolving behind a door of tinted glass, their arrival heralded by the sound of a buzzer. And yet the food, as it emerged, always seemed to be a shade of yellow. When Daisy once remarked on this, her father had tapped his temple with his finger, saying, 'Yellow is the colour of the intellect, you know.' She had not known if he was teasing; she still did not. They each had a red paper napkin left over from Christmas. She helped Sam with his, then spread her own on her knee and Tad dealt another hand.

They had been in bed for many hours when Daisy sat upright. The red numbers on the digital clock beside her were large and oblong and flashed up 02:55.

Tad was singing noisily downstairs. She could hear the slurred and too-familiar words of his favourite song, "Jolene".

Sam still slumbered in the other bed. She wondered how he could sleep when the music was so loud. Daisy squinted in the darkness; the blacker squares against the wall were photographs. She knew these pictures showed a lady in mink coats and little scarves, her grandmother. Nancy was dead now, but Daisy could remember those times they used to stay with her in France, how they would all sit at lunch together, with the glitter of the sea before them, the million glints of silver that bounced and sparkled off the waves. That was a landscape of delicious promise: the hot and dusty scent of lavender, the cherries bright like porcelain upon the table, the tablecloth a thick embroidered linen. But Tad's singing smashed into her thoughts and the memory was swept aside.

Daisy hated country music, hated the lilt of it, the self-pity and the drama. Tad always put it on when he was drinking and sang along to songs of loss and heartbreak, dancing solo on the carpet and crying to ballads of lonesome men and cheating wives. Whenever she heard it, Daisy felt the panic clamber up inside her. She had to, *had* to turn it off right now. It was the middle of the night. She ran downstairs until she reached the doorway to the drawing room and then she paused and wavered, feeling slight and unimportant in her nightie and her naked feet.

Cindy was speaking but her voice was different to before; it had lost its tease and charm and now she sounded desperate. 'Please, Tad. I'm going to help you up the stairs. You've got to get to bed.'

Daisy walked in with her back straight and head high and said the sentence she had rehearsed in her clearest strongest voice: 'Dad. You need to turn the music off. I can't get to sleep.'

But even as the words came out, she felt she saw them tumble to the ground. It was useless; the scene was too familiar. An empty Jack Daniels' bottle stood amidst the fluttered debris of cards, as if someone had tried to do a magic trick but given up halfway. A tumbler of wine lurched against a cushion. And the pale rug was smudged where ash had fallen, like a small animal had left its footprints in the snow. Even though the furniture was in the same place as before, Daisy felt as if everything was upside down and broken into pieces. Tad was crawling on the carpet, a cigarette dangling from his lips, eyes half shut, moaning to the music. When he saw Daisy, he raised one hand and made a pawing motion in her direction. 'Grrr.' He shook an imaginary mane. 'Hey, pussy cat. Come and join this old lion.'

Cindy was standing barefoot and her shirt was half undone, revealing large pale breasts inside a black lace bra. She was not so tall without her shoes on. Her eyes looked frightened as she turned to Daisy. 'I'm sorry.'

'Why don't you just go to bed, Dad?' Each time this happened, she was embarrassed by him, appalled that this drunk man could be her father.

'Come on, Daze, don't stop the party. It's party-party time.' He sat up and crossed his legs, 'You can join in. We can dance, oh yes, sir, we can boogie, boogie woogie, all night long. Cindy, let's have that Cointreau.'

Daisy suddenly understood what was happening: Cindy was about to go.

'I'm sorry, Daisy. I don't know how to help here.' She spread her hands in front of her. 'I mean, it's not so fun, really.'

'We don't need her, do we, Daisy?' Tad shut his eyes and rocked from side to side. 'She can fuck off back to LA if she thinks she's too good for us. Fucking sunny surfer land, full of no-good bums and losers. Movie people. Shallow users.'

'He's always like this when he's drunk. It's okay. Please could you stay just until he goes to bed. I swear, I promise...' But Daisy did not know what she was promising. She did know this would often last for three days solid and that she wanted Cindy please to stay. Tad stood up now and seized Daisy by the hands swinging her limp arms left and right in time with the music.

'Come on, Tad.' Cindy placed a hand on his shoulder. 'Why don't you go fix me that Cointreau.'

Tad let go of Daisy and her arms flopped to her sides. Then he stumbled into the kitchen where they heard a smash as a stool fell over onto the tiled floor.

'But you can't go. Please.' Daisy heard a tremble in her voice. She could not cry. She would not allow it.

'Honey. Quick.' Cindy gave her a gentle push, 'Get on up to bed now. I'll see you in the morning, I'll make you real American pancakes.'

They could hear Tad from the kitchen. 'Whores all of them. Your mother is a whore. Fuck her. Fuck you, Anna, and that fuck-ing ponce you're going to marry.'

'Go on. Go on up.'

So Daisy obeyed, but just as she was passing through the door, she turned back and saw that Cindy was bent over, slipping on her shoes.

Finally the night dissolved. It always amazed Daisy how reliable this fact was; night would eventually depart and morning would arrive and take its place. Whatever happened in the world, the days would keep on coming. By now the music was faint and she could hear the first round of birds outside making louder proclamations, announcing their presence to the world. A strip of milky light seeped through the gap above the curtains.

'Sam,' she whispered. But still her brother slept on. Maybe he did it on purpose. Somewhere in that long night, she must have slept as well. The turmoil and the dread were buried and unreal, the music unimportant. A bus was rumbling down the street and she was thankful. Daisy would go downstairs and rescue Tad, for, after all, this was her role; who else was there to do it?

Because she had prepared herself, Daisy did not mind the scene that she encountered when she set off on her rescue. The music was still playing, and the television was still on, but all it showed was repeating fizzy waves of multi-coloured static. Tad was on the floor, in the position they had recently been taught in their first-aid class at school, the Recovery Position. He was dribbling, but there was no sick pooled into the carpet this time. Since her parents had split up, that was how Daisy usually found him, with a halo of drying vomit round his head. She knew he rearranged the furniture to hide the stains. First she pressed the power button on the stereo so the music stopped, then she crept towards her father and struggled to wrench off his boots. He did not stir. Then, just as she was dragging back the curtains, he rolled and grunted.

'It's okay, Dad. It's morning now.' She heard her own voice and it sounded professional and cheerful, impressive, like a teacher.

'Daisy, help your poor old father into bed. Alka Seltzer.'

Daisy knew the drill by now and so she stood firm in order that Tad could lean on her shoulder like a wounded soldier in the war, and in this way, with her supporting him, they made slow progress up the stairs until they reached his room. There was Cindy's brush and Ellnett hairspray on the chest of drawers.

'Dad, Cindy left. I don't think she's coming back.' Daisy doubted that the glimpse of Californian sunshine she had offered would touch their lives again. So she helped her father into bed and covered him with the navy duvet and pulled the blind and tiptoed out.

There was no more poker after that, and no more girlfriends and the rest of the stay with their father slid by like a mild and unimportant dream. Whole mornings slipped past, wide and promising with summer light, while Tad just slept and Daisy and Sam read books and watched videos. The *Star Wars* movie never happened, so instead they went through Tad's Western collection, watching *Bring Me the Head of Alfredo Garcia* and *The Outlaw Josey Wales*. They saw Tad's only successful film, *Coyote Daze*, and the one that bombed, *Blood in the Sand*. Daisy was amazed that people could enjoy such violent films, that they would pay to watch the hero slicing into someone's stomach with his dagger in *Coyote Daze* and standing as the blood drained out.

Instead of ordinary meals at ordinary times they ate tubes of Pringles and drank Five Alive. When they were really bored, they would stand on the balcony, flicking honey-roasted peanuts onto people's heads below. Sometimes, though, Tad would bounce up and play them songs on the guitar or teach them how to do a handstand, then walk across the room on their hands. But most of all, Daisy wished that they could go outside so she could take Sam to the playground like the other children in the square.

And then it was over, the days had miraculously happened and Anna was coming to pick them up. Daisy could tell that they were all relieved. Tad was extra cheery, and when they left he presented Sam with a book on fighter planes and Daisy with a pair of pale pink ballet shoes, sitting in a nest of tissue paper.

'But Dad, you *know* I gave up ballet last term,' Daisy told him as she climbed into the taxi.

Maybe Tad didn't hear her, because instead, he waved with both hands, like someone signalling a plane, and they waved too, until they turned left at the end of the street and then he was out of sight.

Janet Colson

Patrick's Place

MARTINA DROVE FOR A FEW MILES PAST WHEAT FIELDS AND RUST-COLOURED barns with steep, arching roofs. The sky had clouded over and the route dipped under a denser cover of trees. Agnès had been right about the spring leaves. The greens were fresh and vivid and almost as various as the fall shows that brought out the day-trippers in the weeks following Labor Day. A swathe of forested parkland opened up on the rolling slopes and she could hardly take her eyes off the riot of lime and emerald and the black of the pines. She had to force her concentration back to the road.

When it levelled again, she saw the church. It was a brick building, a metal cross scoring the landscape, angular and incongruous, but it had to be right. A Ford pick-up stood on the shale in front.

Patrick hadn't said what car he drove and she hadn't expected a pick-up. Maybe it wasn't him. She came to a standstill, leaving the engine running. A man got out of the cab and for a moment she didn't recognise him. The beanie pulled over his hair gave him a rugged, unfamiliar look. She tightened her grip on the wheel, fighting an impulse to drive away, but he waved at her and she killed the engine instead. She watched him move cat-like towards her. He leant against the side of her car and she rolled down the window.

'Hey,' he said, leaning in to kiss her on the cheek. 'So far, so good.'

His woody scent shot through her like a charge. Christ, she'd missed him.

Martina followed him to a turn-off and up a bank. Driveways appeared on either side. She wished she could get beyond this nervousness, the strangeness of the roads, the not knowing how his place would be. They came to a shingled house surrounded by pine trees and hemlocks. The windows poked out like cuckoo clocks from the eaves and when she saw a sailboat, she imagined it must be Patrick's place and she let her foot hover over the brake, but he drove on. Eventually he slowed down and hung a left by a post with a battered mailbox. The narrow track seemed to go on and on, until at last they reached a clearing. The clapboard cottage was set back; a large wisteria, not yet in bloom, had knitted itself around the overhang of the porch. He parked next to a boat trailer and she tucked the Subaru in behind.

He leapt out of the cab and took her bag from the trunk. The fly-screen creaked shut behind them as he showed her in. She watched him hang up his jacket and put her bag by the narrow staircase. He placed his hand on the small of her back and ushered her into the kitchen. It felt warm from the range and smelt of yeast and cinnamon. A jar of strawberry jam stood open on the breadboard, copper pots hung on hooks, a worn pine table filled most of the room.

He pulled out a chair for her and she sat facing a door half-open onto a sun-porch. She could see the arm of a couch, a turntable and a few record sleeves scattered across the floor.

'How about coffee?' he said, the Canadian 'oo' sounding in his vowels. 'Or tea?' he went on. 'You okay? You seem tense.'

'I'm good,' she said, not quite sure if she meant it. 'Coffee sounds great.'

He put the pot on the stove and pulled up a chair next to her.

'Welcome to my place,' he said, taking her face in his hands and kissing her on the mouth.

She felt herself soften as his lips nudged hers apart, his finger stroking the side of her cheek. She kissed him back, re-learning the fullness of his mouth, the briny taste of his tongue on hers. The smell of the coffee pulled him away and he got up to flip off the flame. She watched him, his long, pliant fingers winding round the handle of the pot. He spread the other hand on the counter, the muscles in his arm flexing under the soft denim of his shirt. She prayed he wouldn't turn round, not yet, not until she'd studied his neck and how his hair, the colour of maple syrup, curled at his collar. He moved with languid ease and as he shifted his weight from side to side, his buttocks rounded under his Levi's.

When he turned, she kept her eyes on him. He met her gaze and put the coffee pot back on the stove. She went to him, pressing her body against his. She buried her face in his neck, kissing him, finding her way to his mouth, clasping the hair at the back of his head. She felt him hard against her. She put her hand on his belt with no other thought than to feel him inside her. He pushed his hand under her sweater and folded it over her breast. She felt her nipple harden in his palm, her desire like sharp needles.

'Through there,' he murmured, gesturing towards the sun-porch.

She would have taken him on the wooden boards of the kitchen floor, but they made it to the couch. She fell back, kicking off her shoes, him laying down beside her, sliding his hand over her waist and under her jeans. Her body rose towards him with each stroke.

'Now,' she said.

'Not yet,' he said, his green eyes narrowing, 'I want to look at you.'

She felt the cool air between her legs and the heat of his cock on her thigh. She shimmied down lower, pressing herself against him, when a sound from outside startled her.

'It's the wind,' he whispered, his breath warm on her neck. 'It's only the wind.'

He moved, and he was on her, sliding inside her. She gasped. It was like velvet and chocolate and bergamot. She moved with him, rocking until they found a rhythm between them. She felt his heat rise and sweat break on the surface of his skin, the salty taste of him quickening her as his mouth met hers. His spicy scent made her crazy and she wanted to hold on, let it go on forever.

He lay behind her and pulled a blanket from the arm of the couch to cover her. She was warm and weightless, her mind not yet returned. He nuzzled closer and the flesh between her legs throbbed, spontaneous as an afterthought. It was cool in the sun-porch, but from the warmth of her cocoon, only her nose was cold. Beyond the turntable and the stacks of vinyl, the long grass of the lawn blurred into the pine trees at the end, their trunks interlacing into darkness. The wind buffeted against the roof, splattering ragged raindrops onto the glass.

Patrick got up and she lay watching him as he pulled on his jeans and padded through to the kitchen. Her body was peaceful; her mind clear. The rain came down harder, gathering into rivulets where the roof panels met. She followed the drops, each one running its course until they joined and formed patterns as if a spider were weaving its web; the wind whipped against the guttering like a yapping dog. She pulled the blanket up closer round her chin, listening to him as he prepared food: the dull clunk of the faucet, the clatter of a pot on the stove.

'I thought we'd stay home for lunch,' said Patrick, returning with a tray and nudging a wooden beer crate to rest it on.

She sat up and he nestled in beside her, pouring hot tea, then smearing butter onto a thick slice of bread. He smiled to himself as he layered it with ham and cheese – Camembert from a white paper parcel. He gave it to her, sneaking a corner of her cheese as she took it, before piling up another slice.

Her father had loved food, all the food her mother cooked, and Rosa – there was no denying she could cook: the pot roasts, *escalopes* like no restaurant ever made, *dauphinoise* potatoes. No wonder he'd overlooked her foibles. Martina had blown it. Anyone else would have understood, but to leave Rosa waiting was a cardinal sin.

She took a bite from the sandwich, then another. She couldn't remember ever feeling this hungry, or ham that tasted so good, the way it melted in her mouth. 'I forgot to meet my stepmother at The Russian Tea Room,' she said, licking the butter from her fingers.

'How'd she take it?' he said, not missing a beat.

'Hard to say if she'll ever speak to me again.'

'Stuff like that happens to me all the time,' he said, out of the side of his mouth as he ate. 'Something comes up and things go right out of my mind.'

Like the time you went sailing and didn't call, she thought.

'What made you forget?' he said. He passed her tea to her, looking her in the eye like he knew it mattered. He was consoling, though she didn't think she deserved it.

She cupped her hands around the mug, enjoying its warmth. 'Something came up at work,' she said, wiping a crumb from the edge of her mouth.

'What?' he asked, gentle, but persistent.

She brought the drink to her lips, the heat of the steam rising like a blush over her cheeks. She hadn't meant to tell him.

'The bank's stopped paying for my classes at the college,' she said. 'It's just their excuse to get rid of me.'

'I thought this kind of thing only happened to me!'

'You mean they're firing you, too?' she said with a wry smile.

'Not Vassar,' he replied. 'Not yet, anyhow. Back in California, in the good old days.'

'Gary said you were a free spirit.'

He tossed his head back in a full-throated laugh, resting his mug on the crate for fear of spilling it. 'Did he now?' he said, his eyes glittering emerald from the fan of his smile lines. 'I guess that's one way of putting it.'

He said he'd spent too much time on his sailboat, refused to lick enough faculty ass, but there was a glimmer of something else, another reason he'd had to leave. As she watched him drape the last piece of ham over the bread and slice it in two, she remembered what Gary had said about Cynthia, that she and Patrick were old friends, but it didn't ring true. Martina felt sure there was more to it than that.

'Do you like the job?' he said, holding out the bread and ham for her to eat.

She bit into the floury crust, then took it from him.

'Not really,' she said.

'Well, screw 'em,' he said, kissing her with his buttery mouth.

She kissed him back, tasting the copper tang of tea. She noticed the light catching the yellow flecks at the centre of his irises and the way the freckles merged into the pale skin of his lips. Still holding her, he put the lunch things aside and, turning, pinned her to the sofa, whispering all the while in her ear so she giggled and drew him closer.

The wind had calmed, the rain clouds given way to the nacreous gleam of weak sunlight. The afternoon stretched before them. His kisses were playful, coaxing her as he would a child into a game.

'Take me upstairs,' she said, catching his face in her hands as if to still him.

And as he gathered the blanket around her and led her up to the bedroom, Manhattan seemed a long, long way away.

Susan Oke

The Homecoming

CHAPTER ONE

DUSAN JOINED THE QUEUE OF PEOPLE SEEKING ONWARD PASSAGE TO THE CENTRAL worlds. It was hot and airless in the arrivals hall and the queue hardly seemed to move at all. It had taken two days for the message to reach him. For two days he had been bereft of a father and had not known it; the thought left him feeling cold, empty, lost.

His throat tightened as he relived that moment of agonised hesitation outside his father's study.

Caught by the light slicing across the darkened corridor he sees his father engrossed in another of his ancient manuscripts. An aura of intense concentration mingled with excitement emanating from his father's mind brings a ghost of a smile to Dusan's lips. Only his father could find old books exciting. He places one hand against the door and then snatches it away, stepping back into the darkness as his father yawns and rubs his eyes, raising his head to look at the door, a puzzled expression on his face.

He'd left his family home without a backward glance. Thick with anger and resentment, tainted with refuted guilt, he'd stuffed a few essentials into a bag and stalked out of the house. In his heart he knew his father had been the one person who could have persuaded him to stay. That was the last time he'd seen his father alive. Grief and guilt expanded in his chest making it difficult to breathe.

He had been away for five years; it was a lifetime.

I didn't even say goodbye.

With his backpack slung over one shoulder Dusan shuffled and sweated in silence along with the rest of the travellers, teeth gritted against the sense of urgency that fretted and stabbed at him. Security at spaceports, even on a backwater planet like this one, was tight and enforced with harsh efficiency; no one wanted trouble. The rest of his belongings, enough clothes for a week, his favourite weapons and a birthday gift for Felan, were being shipped separately and at this rate would probably arrive before he did.

Finally, it was his turn. Scowling at the security camera, Dusan thrust his left forearm into the ident-scanner and the locking mechanism clicked into place around his wrist. He watched as the information stored on his ident-chip appeared on the screen.

Name: Dusan-Dyn Hoyt

Planet of Origin: Dalshanna

Occupation: Senior Officer, starship Vitra, mercenary class.

Current status: Active

Sub-category: Extended leave of absence

The rhythmic blinking of the cursor on the screen counted out the seconds as he waited for his identity to be crosschecked and verified. It was only when his arm was released and the security barrier slid aside that he realised he'd been holding his breath.

Dusan was born Cathan of the Dakon Family, the third and youngest son of the line of Valard-Medea, one of the most powerful pairings on Rycella, his true home planet. Taller than most, slender and muscled, it was his milk-white hair, pale almost translucent skin and deep violet eyes that made him stand out. Dusan-Dyn Hoyt was his shipboard identity, created for him when he was accepted as a permanent member of the crew of the Vitra. According to ship records he was a native of Dalshanna, a respected member-planet of the confederation of central worlds. His physical characteristics were sufficiently similar for him to pass a visual inspection and Brin, their Comms Officer, was a genius when it came to hacking central world systems. Dusan-Dyn Hoyt existed in the data streams that flowed between worlds; the planet Dalshanna accepted him as one of their own.

He cast a practiced eye over the untidy queues for the three body scanners. The closest included a couple of family groups, their children playing a squealing game of tag in and around the other travellers. In the next, he spotted the feathered crests of a young couple from Praxia. Their race was notoriously claustrophobic – by the way they clung to each other it was clear that they were already beginning to panic. Dusan opted for the longest queue, comprised mostly of solitary travellers; he would be through and out into the departure hall while those families were still trying to round up their kids.

Much later, he'd discovered that in the language of his crewmates 'Dusan' was the name of a pale skeletal demon used to frighten children into behaving, but no one would tell him the meaning of 'Hoyt'. Whenever he asked they would just laugh uproariously and slap him on the back, the casual strength of their bulky muscular frames threatening his balance. The memory sparked a smile that almost reached his eyes; he missed their bad-tempered, unruly camaraderie.

The deception made all their lives simpler. His Vitra ID allowed him to work and travel amongst the central worlds and after five years the persona had become a comfortable and reassuring fit. The natives of Rycella rarely travelled; the central worlds made it clear they were not welcome. People, on the whole, were afraid of telepaths.

Dusan stepped into the body scanner and the door slid closed behind him. The chamber was about five strides long with a sealed door at each end. Almost twice his height and wide enough for three men. It reminded him of the airlock on board the Vitra; only here the matt-grey walls were crammed with sophisticated sensors that could be calibrated to detect any form of weapon or contraband goods. The manufacturers claimed their scanners were foolproof, and they were, except against someone with his talents. He walked through the scanner with confidence, having long ago perfected the art of masking the presence of his personal crystals. And he never went anywhere without his throwing knife, nestled against the inside of his right forearm, held in place by a tightly woven telekinetic net. The opposite door of the scanner slid open and he stepped out into a cavernous concourse that stretched into the distance on either side.

The deafening buzz of thousands of minds emitting an endless stream of chatter stunned him. It was like a physical blow, ravenous in its intensity. His senses were inundated by a cacophony of insistent muttering and urgent whispers, pierced by raucous shouts and bright panic-stricken cries. Dusan focussed on his telepathic shielding, tightening its lattice pattern into a mesh fine enough to filter out most of the noise. He took a moment to get his bearings and then strode off in search of suitable transport; he had a long journey ahead of him.

Captain Vasuk had dropped him off as close to the commercial transport routes as the Vitra's flight plan would allow, but he was still stuck in a minor system on the wrong side of the galaxy.

He quickened his steps and scanned the lists of scheduled flights scrolling along the bright surface of the departure wall. Black text climbed in a slow continuous scrawl from floor to ceiling, the information for each flight delineated by sharp blue vertical lines. This was one journey he had never intended to make. How could he face his Family after what he had done? He knew what they believed of him and although the bulk of the accusations were false, at the core he knew he was guilty. He had shamed his Family and for that reason alone he should never return. Shards of memory taunted him... of his mother crimson with fury at his latest debacle; his brother's final ultimatum; that look of frustrated resignation on his father's face.

Now, here he was, raking through the departure lists, frantically searching for the quickest way to intersect the major trans-galactic trade and passenger routes. Skipping past the local in-system flights Dusan concentrated his search on the less frequent, long haul destinations.

There... the Txeru leaving for Bahram in less than an hour... Gate 6... I can just make it.

It was Anisa, his mother's companion, who had sent the message about his father's death. Dusan had listened to her halting words, stared at her red-rimmed eyes, as the message played out.

He had not wanted to hear it, as soon as he saw her face he'd wanted to turn the recording off. But he didn't. He'd stood, unable to breathe, unable to move until she'd finished speaking. Every word, every grief-soaked nuance a blow he thought he would never recover from.

The words marched through his mind in vicious repetition... *your father is dead... a riding accident... I... we thought you had a right to know... your father is dead... dead...*

It was possible that his mother was too distraught to record the message, but he knew her too well to believe that. No, the way he'd been told was a message in itself. He had simply been informed of the death; he had not been asked to return.

Anisa, you were more of a mother to me...

Dusan had his own reasons for leaving Rycella; quite separate and distinct from the scandal that had forced his hand, they were equally compelling. He had always believed he'd made the right choice, both for himself and for his Family. No one expected him to stay away for long. How could he? Telepaths are communal creatures; they need the company of their own kind. The unbearable isolation should have driven him back home. Even the Crystal Technicians who worked in the Rycellan space docks installing and maintaining the crystal systems in off-world ships travelled everywhere in pairs.

He was not immune to the loneliness. Visited in those dark hours deep into his sleep cycle, when memories have a life of their own, those he treasured would unfold their pain and longing, leaving him staring wide-eyed into the dark. Those were the times when the subliminal hum of the Vitra's systems failed to comfort, and he was acutely aware of the silence that surrounded him. The accumulated ache, the yearning etched into every cell of his body, would make him cry out, desperate to feel the bond once more, to truly belong. And then, despite the crushing futility of the effort, he would stretch out his senses to encompass the ship and the dull unresponsive minds it contained, pushing further and further out into space, searching, hoping. Until, his body drenched in sweat, gasping with the strain, he collapsed back in on himself.

Once, he thought he'd felt an answering touch, the faintest caress of a reply. But the Vitra had been on the very outskirts of the galaxy, taking an intentionally circuitous route through unpopulated and un-travelled space; a response was impossible. It was his imagination, the first sign of the madness that afflicted any telepath isolated from his community for too long.

Talen would find him prowling the decks, dark-eyed and dangerous. As an empath, sensitive to the emotions of others, Talen always knew when his protégé was in trouble. Back in Talen's quarters they would sit cross-legged on the floor, knees touching, hands clasped. Gentle as a breeze, Talen would slip inside his fractured defences, projecting a feeling of white-gold serenity that gradually saturated his entire being. His anguished sense of loss would slowly fade, be drained away and replaced by a sense of calm acceptance. The crew of the Vitra were his family now. And it was enough. Talen's presence, just a heartbeat away from the telepathic bond he craved, was enough to keep him sane: until the next time.

It had given him a grim sense of satisfaction to imagine the disbelief and then the outrage of the Family Heads as the weeks turned to months and there was still no sign of him begging and pleading to be allowed back home. After five years everyone, including his own Family, would believe him dead or irretrievably unstable. Nevertheless, he'd despatched an urgent message to his mother claiming his right to attend the funeral. They knew he was coming, but even he did not know exactly when he'd get there.

The concourse disgorged him into the massive dome of the spaceport's central Hub; crammed full of tax-free shops and eateries it tempted travellers to part with their hard-earned credits before boarding their flights. Lips pressed into a hard line, Dusan fought against the flow of the crowd, the noise from so many mouths and minds testing his patience and the resilience of his shields. The wall encircling the Hub continued to display updated flight information, its smooth surface broken by five broad walkways leading to numbered departure gates. On the far side of the Hub, almost directly opposite where he stood, flashed a large green sign: *Gates 1-6*. Dusan stifled a yawn as he made his way around the perimeter, avoiding the hordes besieging the shops, cafes and bars. His body clock was still keyed to shipboard time, for him it was the middle of his sleep cycle.

There was a good chance he'd be arrested and confined the instant he set foot on Rycella. He was no stranger to the inside of a cell; he'd spent more than his fair share of time in the brig of the Vitra, especially in his first year. The thought of what they'd do to him prickled cold sweat in the nape of his neck and set his teeth on edge. All he could hope for was that it would be his brother Kemen and not one of the Kow Healers who would be given the task of determining whether he was mentally and emotionally stable enough to rejoin the telepathic community.

Dusan scowled and shouldered his way past the hesitant and the slow, muttering curses at the knots of travellers milling around the perimeter wall and blocking his path. Too ignorant to read standard Galac, they gathered in clumps, puzzling over their hand-held scanners as they accessed translations of the departure schedule. Hidden sandbanks in the flow of the crowd, they caused swirling eddies of delay that ramped up his frustration to a dangerous level. He could not summon the focus he needed to scan ahead for a clearer route. He was off-balance, locked tight inside his shields, careening through time and events with no sense of control, a crimson haze of insistent fury making everything distant and unreal. Only his final destination mattered. He had to get there in time.

In time for what?

Driven, infected with an unreasoning urgency, Dusan forced his way through the wall of bodies in front of him, the look on his face silencing any protest. He was already too late; his father was dead, gone. But still an unyielding insistent pressure in the back of his mind pushed at him, *hurry, hurry*, as if by being there he could somehow change what had happened.

He saw them, two spaceport security guards watching his bullish progress, their hands resting casually on their holstered stun guns. Dusan slowed, attempting to mimic the infuriating amble that defined the amorphous creature the crowd had become. Grappling with his wildcat anger, he fought down the urge to tear, spit and scratch his way to the departure gate. If the guards challenged him now... He shoved his fists into his jacket pockets, hunched his shoulders, and lowered his head in a futile attempt to become inconspicuous in a crowd where he stood at least half a head taller than most.

One of the guards walked towards him.

No, no, no.

With great effort, Dusan took hold of the shield he used to hide his crystals from the security scanners and spun it around his body, drawing energy from his rose crystal to strengthen and stabilise its effect. He cast his eyes to the ground to hide the telltale glints of silver that betrayed his crystal's power. If anyone noticed, they'd know instantly what he was, and that would cause more trouble than he could handle right now. The guard stopped and scanned the crowds, a confused expression on his face, then he shrugged, turned, and retraced his steps.

Mark Pendry
from The Prodigal Son

1

I STEPPED FROM THE TRAIN AND INTO MY PAST.

It had been almost twenty years since I last stood on this platform and I was none too happy at being dragged back. I stood motionless, with my holdall in my right hand, a rigid counterpoint to the bustling throng around me. I could see the steeple of the cathedral rising above the rooftops of the town, and was reminded of Father Redmond and happier times. Before the storm. Before the killing.

I closed my eyes. I had to stay focused. I couldn't afford any unnecessary diversions, so the trip down memory lane would have to wait. I wasn't sure what the reception would be to my brief return, or what scars I would leave with this time round. But of one thing I *was* certain: before it was over, two people in this town, now living, would soon be dead.

2

The taxi driver dropped me off at Graceland Villas, a small B&B on Hope Street run by Mrs. Clayton, a prim-looking Scottish woman in her mid-to-late sixties. I was diligently filling in the standard guest questionnaire she had put before me.

'And how long will you be staying Mr.....'

'Forbes,' I said. 'And I'm not exactly sure. Probably a couple of weeks. Maybe more. It depends.'

'On what?'

'On how quickly I finish my business.'

'And what business would that be, Mr Forbes?'

I put down the pen and looked up at her. '*My* business, Mrs Clayton.'

To her credit, she blushed and looked away, busying herself by unnecessarily tidying some pamphlets on the reception desk.

'I'm sorry,' I said. 'I didn't mean to be abrupt with you, it's just that...'

'No. *I'm* sorry, Mr. Forbes. I didn't mean to pry. Your business is your business. I was just trying to be friendly, is all. No offence intended.'

'None taken, Mrs Clayton. Which room am I in?'

She referred to her ledger. 'Well, if you're going to be here for a few weeks, I'll put you in the Emerald Room.'

The look on my face must have given me away.

'It was Reg's idea. My husband. He was a big Elvis fan and he thought it'd be a good idea to decorate each room with a different theme.' She turned and took a key from the rack behind her.

'Uh-huh.'

'You know, a Jungle Room, an Egyptian Room, Nautical Room,' she said. 'Daft bugger.'

'What happened?'

'Well, the two of us soon realised our budget wasn't anywhere near as flexible as Reg's imagination. So Reg moped about for a few days and then I came up with the idea to change the name to Graceland, to keep the Elvis connection, you see, and have a more affordable colour-theme to the rooms instead.'

'Ah, the art of compromise,' I commented.

She chuckled. 'Quite. And, I can assure you, essential to a long marriage.' She handed me two keys, attached to a large plastic green fob. 'Are you married, Mr Forbes?'

'Courted, but never caught, Mrs Clayton.'

She smiled. 'Plenty of time; you're still young. Now, breakfast is from seven to eight-thirty. The smaller key is for your room. The larger key is for the front door. It'll be on the latch until eleven o'clock, but I lock it when I go to bed. Would you like me to show you to your room?'

'It's okay, Mrs Clayton, I'm sure I'll find it. I used to be a Cub Scout.' I turned to go.

'Well, it's through the swing doors, stairs on your left, first floor, second door on your right.'

I stopped at the swing doors and turned. 'By the way, what was my room going to be, back in the day, I mean if Reg *had* had his way?'

'The Vegas Room, for the High Rollers. Are you a High Roller, Mr. Forbes?'

'I am now, Mrs C.'

3

In order to justify the title of The Emerald Room, the Claytons had splashed out on patterned green wallpaper, a green chequered duvet cover and pillowcases, green tiles in the bathroom, along with an olive bath, sink and toilet combo. The only thing that looked out of place in the sea of green was the pink toilet roll; the maid was obviously not getting on board with the programme.

There were a couple of framed prints on the wall, the one above the bed depicting a hunting scene with men in bright red jackets on horseback, a pack of hounds swarming at their feet. Both horses and hounds looked agitated and ready to race off to do battle with the rascally old fox. The other picture, on the opposite wall, was what looked to be an unfinished pencil sketch of a little girl carrying a basket of flowers.

I unpacked my few belongings, put my mobile on charge and considered what to do with my Heckler and Koch semi-automatic handgun. After the Dunblane massacre in '96, pretty much all civilian cartridge-based handguns had been outlawed. So I figured it would probably not be a good idea to wander around the streets of Nottingham with it. Not just yet, at any rate. I forced open the wooden panel at the base of the wardrobe and carefully put both the gun and holster in the narrow space beneath.

After a cold shower to freshen up after my long trip and a change of clothes, I set off for the police station.

4

The desk sergeant was a tall man in his mid-fifties, sporting a full black moustache and a dodgy comb-over. Judging from the grey hair, I guessed the moustache was out of a bottle. Quite why someone one would go to the trouble of dyeing their moustache but not the hair on their head, seemed odd. I toyed briefly with the idea of asking him outright, but he didn't look like someone who smiled much, so I guess it would have to remain another of life's mysteries.

'How may we help you, Sir?' he asked.

'My name is David Forbes.'

He nodded. 'I see, and what's the purpose of your visit?'

'My sister was Greta Royce,' I said. 'She was killed in a hit-and-run in February, and I want to speak with the officer in charge of the investigation.'

He nodded again and produced a notepad and pen. 'And when exactly in February was this, Sir?'

'February 10th. In Tanner Street.'

'That's almost three months ago?'

'Yes. I know. I've been working abroad for the last few years, and out of contact for the most part.'

He wrote something else down on the pad before him and then looked back up. 'Have you got any form of identification on you, Sir?'

I reached into my jacket pocket, pulled out my battered passport and handed it to him. He carefully examined the passport, checked my photo and then looked back up to my face for a moment, then back again at the passport photo.

'I decided to shave it off, but it's still me, though.'

He wrote something further on his notepad and then handed me back my passport.

'And you say your sister's name was Greta Royce?'

'Yes. Greta Claire Royce. She was thirty-six years old.'

'Married?'

I shook my head. 'No. Divorced. No kids.'

The desk sergeant finished scribbling his notes then looked back up.

'Very good, Mr Forbes. Please take a seat in the waiting room and I'll see who's available.'

I made my way towards one of the uncomfortable-looking chairs in the waiting room and sat down. It didn't disappoint. I took a long look around, at the myriad of posters and pamphlets on display, from extolling the virtues of the Neighbourhood Watch, to some disturbing ones on the horrors of domestic abuse and drink driving; via a smiling black police officer in full uniform, promoting ethnic diversity within the police force; to tips on ways to make your house safer and less desirable to burglars. Prompted by the beaming smile of the uniformed black officer in the poster, I was halfway through the pamphlet on ethnic diversity, when the desk sergeant returned.

'It was DC Clarke who dealt with your sister's case. He says he can give an update on her case now, if you'd care to follow me.'

I stood and followed the desk sergeant through a side door and along a series of corridors to a door marked simply Room 315. The desk sergeant opened the door for me and gestured for me to take a seat.

'DC Clarke will be with you shortly.'

With that, he closed the door behind him, presumably returning to the front desk to keep the hordes at bay.

It was a plain room, one table with a phone on it, two chairs and more posters on the walls. There were no filing cabinets, drawers or personal effects anywhere. As there was nothing else to capture my attention, I resumed my scrutiny of the posters. The black officer was still beaming back at me, which I found vaguely reassuring. But this was countered by a rather disturbing NSPCC poster: a stark black-and-white photo of a toddler in a cot cowering in fear, before the shadow of some unseen menace which had entered his room. I felt an involuntary wave of nausea wash over me, leaving a film of perspiration that hadn't been there moments before. I knew that it shouldn't still affect me, not after all this time and distance, but my subconscious obviously hadn't got the memo. I felt dizzy and sat down, gripping the arms of the chair to steady myself. I shut my eyes tightly and tried hard to push old familiar negative thoughts from my mind. My heart was hammering in my chest and my breath became short and laboured. Fuck! Come on! Get a grip! It's been over eighteen years. I'm not the same person I was back then. I can't let it affect me. Not now.

'Are you okay, Mr Forbes?'

I looked up to see a man in his mid-forties, standing just inside the doorway, holding a manila folder.

'Yes, I'm fine,' I said, getting up to shake his hand. 'Sergeant Clarke, I presume?'

'Detective Sergeant, actually,' he replied, looking at me with his head slightly cocked. 'Would you like a glass of water?'

'No. Thanks.'

'Tea? Coffee?'

'No. Really. I'm fine.'

'Fair enough.' He gestured for me to sit, so I did.

He was about my height, approximately 6' 4", with broad shoulders and short black hair. He wasn't in uniform but was smartly dressed in a black suit with a pale blue shirt and a dark blue tie to match.

'And you were the person in charge of investigating my sister's death?'

He nodded. 'That's correct. I was.'

I noticed the thick manila folder which DS Clarke had placed on the table between us. I could make out my sister's name, followed by a long Case number and the word 'Deceased' stamped on it. I felt my pulse start to rise again and took a deep breath.

'So, detective, can you fill me in on what happened?'

'First things first, Mr Forbes. I just need to take down a few details about you, if I may.'

'What do you want to know?'

He produced an A4 notepad from the folder in front of him and took a pen from his inside jacket pocket. We went through the basic stuff: full name, age, and current contact details, then he put the pen down and looked me directly in the eye.

'And where were you when your sister was killed, Mr Forbes?'

'Why? Am I a suspect?'

He smiled. 'Not at all. It's a question that we have to ask. It's not intended to cause offence. Although, I must admit that I am rather curious to hear the answer. We tried very hard to get hold of you at the time, to let you know what had happened, but you appeared to have fallen off the face of the planet. No one knew where you were, nor how to get hold of you. We found both a mobile number and an email address for you in your sister's address book and left several messages, but we never received any replies. I even placed a call to Special Ops to try and trace the phone signal but it was blocked. Which we all found a little odd.'

His eyes were still on mine, but I comfortably held the gaze.

'I move around a lot with my work, detective, and, well... I'm not exactly one for keeping in touch.'

'And what line of work would that be, Mr Forbes?' He'd picked up the pen, which now hovered over the pad, ready to commit my story to print. For one brief moment, I was tempted to tell the truth and say that I kill people for a living. That *Death* was my line of work, that I go to some of the most God-forsaken hell-holes on the planet and do very bad things to very bad people.

'I'm an independent security consultant,' I said. 'I work all over the world, but over the last few years, I've tended to spend most of my time in Asia and the Middle East.'

He made a note on his pad.

'And where were you on the 10th February?'

I was starting to lose my patience. 'Look, I don't want to be rude. But my sister is dead. She hasn't lost her bloody handbag or locked herself out of her flat. She's dead. So, with all due respect, I'd appreciate it, if you'd stop scribbling on your fucking pad and give me some answers.'

DS Clarke sat back in his chair and surveyed my face.

'I understand that you're upset, Mr Forbes. But talking to me like that isn't going to get you anywhere. Do you want me just to walk out and call this meeting at an end?'

I resisted the overwhelming urge to reach across and slam his face down onto the solid table-top and instead took a few deep breaths. 'Japan,' I said. 'I was in Japan. Does that offer of a cup of coffee still stand?'

'Of course,' he said. 'How do you take it?'

Atalanta Miller

A Cloudless Day

'STAY IN JAPAN,' CHRISTOPHER HAD WRITTEN TO THEA. 'TAKE A SABBATICAL, MY dear; we want you back in six months, not before and not after.' She felt his presence bounce off the page. His protective eye caressed the flimsy paper with words and this time she was happy for them, relieved to have the chance to live in Japan. She pictured him waving his enormous, long arms across his room; pointing a Michelangelo finger at her, surrounded by his immense library, books spilling from the shelves, spreading out to form a carpet of letters over his floor; and quietly, pointedly, saying, 'Look after yourself. Write, and come back to see us when you're ready.'

Thea settled into a routine of love, literature and letters in the postage-stamp-sized village of Shobara–shi. She moved in with Guy in his Western-style studio with its fancy loo that played music at every flush and blew hot air at your bottom. She broke the precious rice cooker early on, got hammered on sake and passed out under a table at a local eatery, and she learnt to bowl, play golf and murder hopelessly bad karaoke songs with Guy.

After a few weeks she managed to start earning her keep by teaching English. Her favourite student was the unconventional Buddhist priest, Reverend Dokyo Takamitsu. This man was a nineteenth-generation Buddhist priest and he radiated positivity. He was quite tall for a Japanese man, had a celestial face, a thick mop of shiny straight black hair and almond eyes that beamed behind wire-framed glasses. He reminded Thea of a holy Cheshire cat.

After class one evening, Thea asked Reverend Takamitsu whether he would give a memorial blessing to mark the anniversary of her sister's death. She thought that Helen would approve and appreciate the poetry of her soul being remembered in a rural temple, in the heart of a Japanese country village. Takamitsu looked deep into Thea's eyes and said of course he would.

The first year anniversary was extremely important in the Greek Orthodox Church. Thea knew she would be letting her family down by not being with them when they gathered around the graveside in Switzerland. Omy, Delphine and Celeste would brave the loss together; she pictured them holding hands. But Helen would have wanted her to follow her heart, follow her dreams.

It was a relief to have a focus on the day; somewhere physical to go to and some place to reach for, to take her out of her guilt for not being with her family and to stop the grief from overwhelming her, a young girl swimming in a tsunami, trying to surf a wave far bigger than she could manage.

The more she thought about it, the more perfect it seemed to head for Takamitsu's temple; to have a floor of privacy for her tears to fall on, prayers to heaven each and every one.

The tidy pavement led her to the top of the hill. The street narrowed just past the bakery on the corner, the one with the finest cucumber and egg sandwiches, the crusts cut off and presented with delicate artistic delight. The smell of vanilla sugar came from warm doughnuts being put in cardboard boxes for children's teatime snack – far more delicious than any she had ever tasted. Today she could not think about taking a bite of one. Her feet took her past the bowling alley; the golf range; the karaoke bar; 'Joyful', the supermarket; and away from the smells of miso soup wafting from the restaurants and the curdling aroma of boiling sea weed and salty fish. Finally she came to the garden near Takamitsu's house and his temple.

Rae, Takamitsu's wife, was outside sweeping their front steps and put down her brush to take Thea's hand. Rae kissed Thea on the cheeks. Both women bowed and smiled at each other as they each bent lower in their greeting. Eventually Thea stopped and laughed.

She followed Rae into the house. They sat drinking tea and talking. Rae lifted the iridescent porcelain teapot high, letting the light catch the flower and the duck-egg blue of the blossom on the finely painted teapot, and they reverentially watched the clear water stream into the petite handle-less cup, a few petals of the flower breaking its flow before releasing into the cup. The scent of the flower drifted between them. Rae could have been performing in *Madame Butterfly* at the Royal Opera House, so timeless and elegant were her movements.

Takamitsu came into the room at that moment and Thea jumped up to bow her greeting. He was not in his usual jeans and sweatshirt but in his formal robe, a *donjiki*. It was a rich vermillion with a gleam of burnt umber, and covered in a delicate silk weaving of chrysanthemums. She had never seen him formally dressed before. He looked like the holiest, kindest man she could hope to know.

'I am sorry to keep you, Thea. Let's go now into the temple.'

She started to follow him and remembered the flowers Rae had given her to take as an offering to the Buddha. She had been briefed quickly and she was embarrassed not to have brought them herself.

'Don't worry Thea, how are you to know our customs?' Rae, with quintessential dignity and gentleness, explained that as a chief mourner you could bring food, drink and flowers to the temple, a virtuous deed to the Buddha, and transfer the merit to the memory of the deceased. 'We believe,' she continued, 'That through these gifts and chanted prayers, all beings, including you, Thea, will attain the Buddhist path.'

'Will you come with me, Rae?'

'No, it's for you to go alone,' Rae replied, 'Dokyo will show you what to do.' She touched her hand and nudged her towards her shoes.

Thea took off the guest slippers and put them in their place by the front door, neatly filed amidst the family's slippers and shoes, which indicated who was in or out of their busy home. She put on her outside shoes and carried the slippers he gave her for the temple. She imagined her grandmother in Switzerland tottering in her high-heeled snow boots, walking towards the real graveside with Celeste and Delphine on either side, propping her up, while she supported them with her survivor's strength. While Thea felt her tears well up all too easily on this day, she knew her grandmother's eyes would be dry. 'If I cry for Helen,' she remembered her grandmother telling her, 'I will never stop.'

Thea followed Takamitsu out of his home and saw his mother waiting for them outside the temple. The Greek priest would be greeting her family now, shaking and kissing hands with solemn devotion. Thea bowed low to Takamitsu's mother and she returned the greeting with respect. Respect for the chief mourner, Thea realised, was a respect she had not shown her grandmother on this unnatural day.

Takamitsu proudly told Thea, 'My mom is eighty-three. And look, so, so strong!' Indeed she was. Her face bore creases of time and laughter but she had the air of youth about her. He left Thea, and his mother took her into the temple and gave her the *gobutsuzen* envelope in which to place some money as an offering for the memorial service. Luckily, Thea had some yen with her and, familiar with the Greeks paying the priests in gratitude for their services, she was not surprised by the custom. They removed their shoes and stood on an ornate *tatami* mat with their hands together in prayer waiting for Takamitsu to arrive. She breathed in a giant breath of air and suddenly the intensity of the spiritual room, the decorations of flowers and fruit his mother had laid out and the sight of this beautiful old lady made her remember again why she was there. How could she forget?

One second Helen was alive and standing, breathing fresh mountain air into her lungs, holding a heavy gaudy crucifix on a lumpy golden chain. The next moment her body was smashed on the ground. A pool of blood would have spread out on the blanket of snow. Dark red against white, a symbol of bad luck. In that moment where gravity shows no forgiveness, no second chance of life, what would Helen's thoughts have been? Were there any? Did calm descend on her clouded vision, an ethereal feeling of being at one with the world when chaos surrounded her? Did her heart shatter with despair as she fell? Did anyone see? Did they try to stop her and shout out, 'NO!'

Or was there just the deafening sound of no one, not a soul? Only a soft wind in the fir trees, a cloudless sky, a bright winter sun in her eyes, the metal of her balcony bars, the cold against her skin, one last time. Nature waited for her, insanity or clear-minded determination pushed her, and thousands of miles away we all screamed. She was so loved and in that second she broke our hearts, as we must have broken hers.

Thea remembered hearing the news. She could still taste the scream of denial in her voice mixed with the bile of despair. She'd locked herself in the bathroom, curled in a foetal ball, rocking, shaking; eventually, she'd stopped screaming and sobbed. And then the comfort of Guy, his presence in the room, arms around her, somehow enfolding her, telling her it was going to be okay. All the people in that tiny flat who'd heard her, who just didn't know where to look, and she felt bad for them, sorry to bring this into their home.

How did she move from the bathroom floor? How did she stop the impossible laugh that shook her? How did she control her wild grief? She had to go to Celeste, get to Switzerland, arrange a funeral, buy an aeroplane ticket and clothes. They bought black jumpers and she was annoyed with the sweet sales lady who took so long and made ridiculous conversation. Celeste had squeezed her arm while Thea fidgeted with grief, waiting to pay for a purchase she had never wanted. She had no idea on that day how this shock would unfold, how many days it would last, how strange it would be to be able to laugh and love and eat when Helen really had gone, had done the impossible and hurled her body over the bars.

'I want to be free from my life!' Helen had said years before. 'Fly like a bird in the sky on a cloudless day.'

Today was a cloudless day, Thea thought. She sat in the temple and swallowed her sobs. She watched Takamitsu walk slowly into the temple and, standing before her, he solemnly asked her to tell him the name of her sister, as was tradition.

She said her name out loud, 'Helen.' Helen, so strong, so beautiful, so gone.

He started to chant the prayers of Buddha to help them come into contact with the heart of his teachings, and he lit incense so the sweet scent purified them as it did in the Greek Church. The smoke rising would take their thoughts to the deceased. Thea kept thinking, as she watched and held her hands together, that Helen would have loved this, and she wanted Helen to be there with them so much that strangely, she felt she was. Thea fought back her tears, feeling shy and proud to be there, and she wanted to be as controlled and calm as these two people before her.

The ancient Japanese prayers, like the Greek ones she was so familiar with, though never sure of their exact meaning, had the same lyrical sounds, the same language of piety, of faith and of an undying love for our souls. Takamitsu's chanting was light and high-pitched compared to the throaty depth of a bearded Greek bishop, but his tone was as solemn. He was devoutly serious and the significance of his words needed no translating. They washed over Thea's bowed head and floated in the misty air. She imagined the chants leaving through the temple doors and reaching the paddy fields around them, floating up to the dense green mountains that encircled this village and, weaving up through the trees, following the birds and the butterflies in God's finest garden to rest somewhere high and unreachable. She prayed her sister and mother could hear them and feel the caress of her love, her longing, her mourning in this Japanese temple miles away from home.

As the service came to an end, Takamitsu said to her in his best English: 'I pray for the soul of your sister, Helen, and today we remember her on the day that she died, one year ago, and we pray for your mother, Anne-Marie, too. May they rest in peace.'

Hearing his pronunciation of their names brought a slow smile to Thea's face. Confused by her tears, through her private prayers to heaven she felt the sun and the rain within her, the everlasting rainbow of their love.

'Thank you, Reverend Takamitsu.' Thea bowed as low as she could. He had helped her to control a grief that had felt as savage as the beast of the second coming slouching towards Bethlehem; to slay a guilt that felt cruel in the extreme; and to attain an equanimity and release into serenity.

'Please, Thea, before you go, have a walk in our garden. Take as long as you want – I have some special water for you to drink from the stream.'

'Really' she asked. 'What is it?' She followed him out of the temple, unconsciously crossing herself three times as she stepped out of the holy place, grateful not to be nodding to a crucifix of a dying Lord Jesus or kissing an ancient icon that felt as cold as death on her lips. God and his Son had not saved the people she loved most. She knew she had a way to go before she could make her peace with them.

As soon as Takamitsu's feet were off the holy steps of the temple they started to bounce again. Thea smiled behind him.

'So, Thea,' he said. 'My mom is eighty-three and you see how young she is today.'

'Yes,' Thea laughed in reply, wondering where this was going.

'And,' he continued, 'my wife, well, she is exceptionally beautiful – yes?'

'Absolutely.' Thea agreed.

'And me Thea – what can I say? I have to be modest, of course. I am a priest, but they say I am very, very intelligent.' He burst out laughing at himself.

'Definitely!' Thea laughed back with him.

'Well, the reason for this is the water in our stream. Come and taste it. You see ancient wisdom, powers and beauty fall on Japan...' He winked at her. 'The mist from the mountains, it drips into the water, it hangs low and thick covering the sky...' he trailed off.

'That's beautiful Reverend Takamitsu. Have you been reading your Wordsworth again?'

'The pantheist lives in us all, Thea. And seriously, it's been said that the water from this stream will give the people who drink it youth, beauty and intelligence. It's a national treasure.'

They walked towards the mirrored stream, grassy and rocky at its edges. The density of green astonishing in its emerald hues.

Beautiful bonsais led the way towards it and a blanket of lush grass spread under their feet.

Tread softly, Thea thought. This is a place of dreams.

Takamitsu had an old ladle sitting on what looked like a stone birdbath, grey and mottled with moss creeping through its cracked edges. He ceremoniously picked it up and scooped a little water from the stream. 'Here, Thea.' He offered her the water to drink as a priest gives the blood of Christ at communion. It was cold against her tongue, fresh and icy, soothing to the heat in her throat.

'Can I take a bottle home, Takamitsu?' She joked.

'Ah, Thea, how rich I could be if I sold this water.'

She stared at him, surprised; he looked like the richest man on earth.

'No, you can't take it home, but you can come and visit me every year and be young, beautiful and intelligent.'

'Sounds like a blessing,' she said.

'I will leave you now. Please send my fondest regards to Guy san.'

'Of course,' Thea said. She watched him leave and walk back up the grassy bank, his temple standing proudly some distance before him, like a castle on a cloud.

Thea sat on a rock, looking at her reflection in the water. It was so still, so utterly quiet in this Japanese garden. She couldn't imagine being anywhere else on such a day. Relief swept through her that she was not in Switzerland, not where it happened. Amidst the sea of green before her there was not a trace of snow nor a single drop of red.

Colette Swires

Neville Rides Out

Neville pulled up outside Hill and Dale, country pursuit outfitters, and as he entered the gloomy store a small brass bell sounded and an elderly assistant emerged from a back room, divided from the shop by a dark red velvet curtain.

'Can I help you, Sir?' he enquired, adjusting the length of measuring tape draped around his shoulders.

'I've been invited to a day's shooting and riding at Hanbury Hall,' Neville announced proudly, followed by a more hesitant enquiry about what exactly he should be wearing.

'Well, Sir, will you be shooting or riding?' he asked, smiling benevolently.

Neville thought for a moment. Recalling a rather humiliating day's clay-pigeon shooting last year during which he had missed every time, he pondered the idea of joining the hack instead. He had a rather rosy recollection of riding at school. The majority of his lessons had been conducted in a ménage, but how different could it be in open countryside? It would be the same technique, after all.

'Kit me out for riding, my man,' he decided firmly.

'Very good, Sir. I would recommend the Harris Tweed.' He cleared his throat and added: 'I think we have a riding coat in your size.'

Neville stood in front of the mirror admiring his reflection. Not bad at all. The riding coat suited him very well. He cut quite a dash in his country tweed. The boots were a little tight and restrictive;

he would have to get used to walking in them without looking like John Wayne. Neville waved the crop and slapped his thigh, wincing with pain and colouring a little at his own stupidity.

As the assistant discreetly announced the total he winced for a second time, produced his wallet and decided to put the amount down to company expenses. It was, after all, an invitation from a country magazine in which his gallery had placed an advertisement. A number of other gallery owners would be attending which would make the event an ideal networking opportunity.

The following morning Neville left the motorway and main roads behind and began to drive through the winding country lanes. Shifting down a gear as he accelerated around a curve in the road, he was afforded an uninterrupted view of the undulating hills and valleys of the Berkshire countryside. Turning off at the sign for Hanbury Hall, his spirits began to soar as he reached the tree-lined avenue, a mile of lime trees and the great house standing imposingly in the distance, its ancient cedars rising majestically in front of the hall.

The head groom welcomed the assembled riding party and the head groundsman was on hand to direct the shooting party. Neville followed the former group towards the stable block. Most of the party appeared to be well acquainted, chatting as they ambled on, affording Neville the opportunity to observe that most of their riding gear appeared to be well worn over what was likely to be years of riding experience. Steeling himself for the task ahead, he was quite aware that animals could smell fear from several paces.

'I think we'll mount you on this trusty steed,' the head groom announced, patting the hindquarters of an enormous bay cob, which appeared to be sagging in the middle. Neville initially balked at the size of the animal, but glancing around at the occupants of the other stables with their wild fiery eyes and furtive movements, he was won over by the look of sheer disinterest in the big lazy eyes of the horse he had been offered.

Neville stood on the mounting block and, holding the reins, took a deep breath and swung his leg, just as the horse walked forward a few steps and stopped. The head groom smiled and stepped forward to hold the horse for him as Neville swung his leg a second time and heaved his bulk onto the horse. A wave of panic surged through him as he realised how far he was from the ground, should he fall. Attempting to banish such thoughts, he announced with confidence, 'Walk on!' then, 'Er, what's the name of my horse?'

The groom spoke languidly, 'Phoenix. He used to be the master of the hunt's horse, until he traded him in for a new model. He's a good old boy, though.' Leaning forward, he patted him on the rump, sending him skidding forwards on the cobbles, causing a rather alarming wobble and a significant degree of anxiety to his rather ungainly rider.

As Neville left the grey cobbled courtyard of the stable block and his horse walked on through the arch, and out onto the open fields, his spirits began to lift. He was relieved to note that although the majority of the hacking party were quite a way ahead, Phoenix, being apparently a fairly uncompetitive horse, was quite unconcerned by the widening gap and was happy to trot at a slow pace. As his horse began to amble amongst the soft ferny carpet of green grass, still damp with melted frost, Neville attempted to match the rhythm and pace of his horse, before resigning himself to bouncing out of time for the rest of the ride. The hazy sunshine of a winter's day filtered through the clouds. Neville gave a contented sigh and since he was apparently quite alone, began to sing an old cowboy song to himself, *'I was born under a wandering star...'*

A few miles back, on the other side of a large bank of twelve-foot hedging running parallel to the field, the local hunt was gathering pace. Although the kennel-huntsman had been instructed to ensure that the trail was laid at a significant distance from the guest riding group, Neville had unwittingly allowed his horse to stray some distance from the hacking route which he was meant to have been following.

He began to realise that he could no longer see his fellow riders; they had completely disappeared out of view. He hadn't really been concentrating on the route which, now he came to think of it, he hadn't remembered to ask about. To his right was a densely wooded area, which he was keen to avoid as he had visions of being unseated by a low branch. As he paused to decide in which direction to head, he heard a low rumble. Glancing up, he noticed in puzzlement that the winter sky was a pale shade of blue, without a rain cloud in sight. However, as he gazed around he realised with a creeping sense of horror that the thundering was coming from behind him and was getting louder. Before he had a chance to gather his wits and determine what on earth could be happening, his horse suddenly took flight.

Neville gave a whimper, leant forward and attempted to grip tightly with his chubby thighs, which, though quite bereft of any sort of riding muscles, merely spurred on Phoenix, who was now galloping towards the group of riders. Neville caught the occasional glimpse of them through the copper beech hedges and the bare branches of the trees. Perhaps he had somehow taken a short cut and caught up with the hack, he decided in relief.

However, to his bewilderment he began to wonder if he could hear dogs howling, and as the group reached the limits of the trees it appeared that quite a number of the party were wearing red coats. Before Neville had a chance to process the full implication of this information, the party which had now come into view, was a short distance ahead, galloping towards a five-foot dry stone wall. Phoenix gave a whinny of pure delight and, recalling his glory days, broke into a faster gallop.

Neville gave a howl of pure terror as he leant forward, and in a state of utter panic, clutched helplessly at Phoenix's mane. As the hunting party sailed over the five-foot wall with ease, Neville could see that he, too, was heading for the same wall at a gathering rate of knots. He moaned and closed his eyes as Phoenix flew over the wall. As Neville landed on the other side, he realised, with a sudden surge of elation, that he was still on his mount. Blinking through the sweat which was beginning to bead on his forehead under his riding hat, he could see Hanbury Hall nestled majestically in the hills just a few miles ahead. Perhaps there was nothing to it after all, he decided triumphantly; he would gallop home following the hunt.

Phoenix, however, had no intention of following the hunt. As the master's former mount, he had been accustomed to riding in front, and with a sudden lurch which threatened to unseat Neville altogether, he continued his flat-out gallop to make up the distance. Clinging on for dear life, Neville realised that he was hurtling towards the members of the hunt at an alarming speed and that his mad, mad horse was not going to stop. He called out, but his thin panicky voice was carried off on the wind. By now, Neville was a few strides away from collision and with a flash of inspiration he called out the only hunting phrase he could call to mind. 'Tally-ho!' he bellowed, as his horse ploughed through the middle of the riders, dispersing them. Overtaking the master of the hunt, Phoenix gave a triumphant whinny, followed by a sudden surge of speed, causing Neville to lose a stirrup and, to his horror, slip sideways. Clinging onto the left side of the mane he slipped further round with every lurch. As Phoenix finally began to slow his pace, he gave a last whinny, reared up on his hind legs and deposited Neville into the hedgerow.

Neville braced himself for the impact, but was not prepared for the sudden rush of cold water as he landed in the muddy ditch at the foot of the hedgerow. Wet, sore, exhausted and humiliated, Neville picked himself up in time to watch Phoenix belt off towards the house, his load considerably lightened.

Neville, with his head hung low, turned and began to squelch back in the direction of his rapidly departing horse, towards Hanbury Hall, attempting to block out the peals of hearty laughter which rang out in the crisp January air.

Meera Ashish

A Package Called Marriage

I WALKED OUT INTO THE COLD WIND AND SWALLOWED HARD, FIGHTING THE TEARS. The chill in the autumn air brushed harshly against my eyes as I walked down Carnaby Street, seeping through my skin as the wind tugged at my open coat.

I was that little girl again, looking up at the sky and praying to the God Dadi had told me about, who lived beyond the medley of grey and blue and white above me, watching all of us. It's all in His hands. Nothing is in our control. Dadi had inscribed those words on my mind - an old saying; something I had chosen to forget.

It was that time late in the afternoon, when glum faces on the street gaze downwards, wondering why the day is already falling into night, cursing the weather, waiting to be in the warmth of their homes, dreaming of curling up on a sofa and sipping hot tea. It was like a perfectly sprayed mist, illuminating the shades of darkening blue, its pointed tips connecting the earth to the heavens. It was speaking, delivering messages, smiling and scowling. Perhaps the same moon was watching Dadi right now, through the window by her bed. I pinched my eyes again and, through the layers of heavy air, of melancholy and inertia, I asked the moon to give Dadi energy and willpower. Tell her to live, please. Please. And then, quickly, a fine whisper of cloud passed over the moon, slicing it in two.

An image of Dadi lying on the hospital bed, a mask strapped to her mouth, with her eyes shut tight and looking white, settled in my mind. Her face, drawn with small, delicate lines, had yielded gracefully to the command of age. Her hands were fragile, her face seemed weak, the thin folds of her lips coiled inwards, as though gravity was pulling down on them. But the content look on her face, the slight hint of a smile just before it appears, gave me some solace.

I passed Liberty's and started pacing toward the station. A dry leaf circulated in a small whirlwind. More than anything else, Dadi hated the weather in London. And she hated how people's moods depended on the weather. From a small leaf to myself, we all have to succumb to its force, happily accepting it in our most favourable times and cursing it when we are let down.

I squashed through the rush of people as I walked down the steps at Oxford Circus station. My phone vibrated. It was Milen. I didn't want to talk about it, but I had to tell him. Perhaps he already knew.

'Hey.'

His tone of voice was too normal. I sighed with relief.

'Milen, I'm just about to get on the tube. I need to talk, but I'll call when I get home.'

I cut it off before he had a chance to reply and switched off my phone. I was too scared to know anything else.

The train grumbled from stop to stop and I sat like a stone, without noticing anything or anyone around me. I felt lost. Drained. As though I had been sick over and over again. As though my blood had been drawn out and the energy in me was emptied. I wanted to be taken care of by Dadi. If only she could take me to bed and stroke my hair again and again. If only she could tell me this was a bad dream and put me back to sleep.

I wondered why I had not sought Dadi's guidance before deciding to marry Milen; why I had not tried to gain her approval, or spoken to her about breaking up with Sunny. She, who would sing a lullaby every day to put me to sleep, until my eyes remained shut; who would always save me a chocolate and give it to me when nobody was looking; who knew that I missed school sometimes just to spend time with her; and who would tell me about the charming and handsome prince that I would marry one day. She had sculpted my young character, and yet I took the most important decision in my life without consulting her. I had told her about Milen and expected her to be happy; and she was – she unreservedly shared my joy.

I ran to the coat stand in the entrance, where my mother had carefully hung my brown coat from one of the higher pegs, and, delving into the deep pocket with its receipts and train tickets and two hair clips, I drew out my mobile. Should I tell Milen I'm going to see Dadi or should I ask him? Did I need to ask his parents? How would he react? The strength of my hope made me quite certain that he would agree once he realised how important this was to me.

Milen's name flashed on my screen as I was dialling his number.

'Hey, I've been trying to call you,' he said in the deep voice I always loved to hear; only now it seemed distant - far removed from the memories slipping through my mind. Each recollection was a different slide in the park, which Ami had taught me to enjoy and slither carelessly down as I grew up. I sat at the bottom of the staircase and leaned forward. My eyes settled, as they always did, on a large faded grey patch which had permanently stained the camel-coloured carpet in the passageway years ago.

'I was just calling you – sorry. I – I - just got home and found –' My words stumbled on the rocky, fragile optimism that was holding me up.

'What? What's happened?'

I felt a few tears roll down my cheek. My lips became salty. 'Milen, Dadi's had a heart attack. I think she's fine, but we don't know much more. She's been taken to hospital and we're just waiting to hear more.' I looked away from the carpet stain, remembering how Sunny had spilt his wine there while trying to wrap his arms around me.

'Oh, Aarti. Oh, God. How did - ? Are you okay? I'm coming over.'

I pressed my head on my fingertips. Perhaps it would lessen the worry, perhaps it would calm my headache. I wanted Milen now. 'Please come, Milen. I really need to talk to you.' I spoke quietly as the living room door stood ajar.

'I'm on my way,' he said.

I watched the drab colours of the living room, which seemed to reflect the dark greys and blues brewing outside. My mother, who was oblivious to my appearance at the door, sat staring at her hands. Her thumbs were circling each other in a constant rhythm. Was it nervousness? For a moment, they were fast, and then they would slow down, as though reflecting the pace of her thoughts. Her eyes were frozen in concentration as she stared down at her slender fingers, which had recently begun to ripen all over with tiny lines.

Just then, my phone rang and startled my mother. I moved into the passageway and hastily picked it up, expecting Milen.

'Hello?'

'Hey... Aarti,' a man's voice hesitantly responded. It was Sunny. Why was he calling me now?

I paused and felt a deep frown knot my brows. 'Mmm –'

'Please – wait – please don't put the phone down on me. Please!' This was not the first time he had called since we broke up, but it had been a few months since our last conversation. I ran up to my room, wanting to be alone. In my rush, I stumbled on the steps and opened my mouth in pain, silently.

'Are you okay, Aarti?' I heard my mother bellow from downstairs.

'Yep,' I replied, holding my phone down so that Sunny would not hear.

'Aarti, I'm... I've been meaning to call you, but just haven't brought myself to... and...'

I closed the door quietly behind me, pushed my hairdryer aside and sat on the bed, on the clothes spread over it, holding my toes and pressing them together. I wasn't sure whether to tell him about Dadi. I wanted to. Yes, yes... I wanted him to comfort me. But then, if he suddenly turned up at the door – he might do that – it would become too messy. It would be too much to deal with right now.

'What?' I demanded. That constant reminder that he was always there; that he wanted me back.

'I know you must be happy... you're.... getting married soon.'
He sounded nervous.

I could feel heaviness in my throat. I closed my eyes and tipped
my head backwards, swallowing the tears. Then I cut him off.

Did he know that everything with Milen and his family was
not as right as I had imagined? I felt so vulnerable now, waiting
to know that Dadi was okay. Why, why did he have to tempt me?
Why did he not understand how difficult it was for me? Somewhere in the post-engagement shrouds of my heart – for during
my engagement, my mother-in-law had torn me apart – I felt a
gloom that matched his. I had dialled his number so many times
since then and cut it off.

He thought that without him I could not be happy. He might
have been right, but the religious difference would have always
been a stumbling point, another reason to argue. When I was with
him, marriage seemed far away; religion didn't matter then. There
was no moderation, never, not with us. We lived on the idealism
of impulse, of passion, a frail sheet which anything that solicited
belief and opinion only tore. But it worked because of the strength
of attraction: because when we were together, nothing existed
but the laughter, the kisses, our bodies, the chatter – just chatter,
and the friendly silences. I was living in a dream. And yet it was
real. It had been real for four years, as intense and heated in our
arguments as it was in our excitements. The only blemish in our
relationship existed in his being a Sikh, and my being a Hindu,
and it was for this reason that I kept it from my parents, which
weighed heavily on us.

Something in his voice, like an old magnet, was pulling me
with familiar warmth. I wanted to call him back. I wanted to
speak to him. But it was wrong. I knew that I was feeling this
overwhelming rupture in myself only because my emotions were
balancing on a rope grazed and worn thin by confusion – and a
sudden fear. Just then, my phone rang.

I held my breath.

Sunny began slowly. 'It's taken me time to decide to call you, and a lot of guts.' He paused. 'And even though I'm meant to be glad for you, that you have found the right person, I just cannot bear the thought of you – being married to another man.' He raced through those last words as though he was admitting to something that was his fault, as though he did not want me to hear it. The film of bitterness that lined his voice burned me. His last words 'another man' rang in my ears as I lay down and wriggled inside my thick duvet, hiding away from light filtering through the large window. The words echoed through the empty halls of uncertainty that suddenly filled my mind. They clanged like the church bells as we entered our school Christmas service, before we sang carols.

I looked through the gap in my duvet and remained still, my eyes fixed on the empty ceiling, on the small area by the door where the white paint was peeling off. My heart, racing, was filled with anger and compassion. Emotions heaved in my throat. I wanted to cry. Could he hear it in my breathing? I held the phone away from my mouth.

He took a long, drawn out breath, pausing to gather more courage. 'Aarti, maybe it's not right that I call you, but I needed to know again why –' and here, his words were arrested, like a galloping horse whose reins have been pulled.

'Aarti?'

I replied with a faint 'Hmm.'

'I – I – just want to know that you're sure. One last time.' He spoke slowly, as though each word had to be carefully chosen and required a certain strength to say. 'Aarti, please – please just think about what you're giving up.'

My eyes shut and, for a moment, I felt his hug – his arms forcing my body against his, his warm breath on my neck. I longed for him. Tears dripped into my hair. I clutched my pillow. I wanted to tell him everything – about Dadi, about my regrets, about the engagement – and I wanted his sympathy.

I turned in my bed restlessly, saw my black silk pyjamas fall on the floor and faced the window. Through the mist of my tears,

I looked at the small statue of Ganesha sitting on my window sill. It was a gift from my mother. 'Ganesha will give you luck,' she had said as I opened it before starting my A-levels. 'Take him with you – Ganesha will bring you luck,' she told me as I left for university. Always, before each exam, she would check that I prayed to Ganesha.

Once, I had used the faithful Ganesha in my fight with Sunny. Maybe I shouldn't have. After all, he was right - I didn't really practice my religion. But then, what was there to practice? And surely that did not mean I could adopt another religion. Surely that did not mean I could be a Sikh. I was not prepared to do that for him, or for anyone. 'I pray to Ganesh,' I told him. 'You've seen the Ganesh in my room – well, I pray to him. I might not go to the temple, but I still pray, and that's what makes me a Hindu,' I said firmly. But that night, I had wondered what it meant to be a Hindu, what it meant to be Indian, and whether it really mattered to me. I felt British more than anything – everything I knew, I had learned from here. I was living and breathing the air of London, I spoke only English, all my friends lived in this country, I was working here and earned in pounds – and yet I was labelled an Indian. I was a British Indian who had no associations with India, who had no idea about what India was and what she stood for. I hated being held in a cavity of uncertainty, trying to answer elusive questions for which I knew I had no answers. It was not for this reason that I had left Sunny - because he was the kind of guy who would have finally given in and let me be a Hindu - but our arguments about religion had made me realise much more about our differences.

My tears had stopped. But had he heard me? Had he caught the current of doubt and pain that chafed my throat, I wondered. For a moment, I wished he had. I wanted him to draw the words out of me. 'I really didn't mean to hurt you, Sunny. You know that –' my sentence got stuck – *baby* was about to tumble out of my mouth, 'but we wouldn't have worked. This really isn't easy for me, especially now. Please try to understand. Being with you was... but we had too many issues, too many arguments and I – I'm –'

'Then why are you crying? You obviously miss me, Aarti.' With the urgency that impregnated his voice, there was also a definite forcefulness, that same forcefulness I knew him so well for, that reminded me of my father – something I never could stand. It brought back so many of the reasons why I decided to end the relationship – Sunny and Aarti – that I had been so sure about for years. That I would be with him forever had been the most certain aspect of my life. We had planned our wedding, we had fought about our children's names – Simmy, Annika or Anya, Raj or Jay – our world map was dotted with all the countries we would visit, and the false rings we had worn on our wedding fingers embodied our commitment.

I swallowed my tears. 'I don't think we should be talking like this – I've made a decision and I'm not going to change it,' I replied sternly. 'I'm getting married in a month.'

'But –'

'But Sunny, it's over!'

An abrupt silence overcame us.

'I'm sorry, Sunny. This is difficult for me, too.'

'Okay, sure.' The curbed tears tainted his voice.

'Take care... good luck,' I spoke with hesitation, not sure what to say. I wanted to tell him something else. I wanted him to probe me with questions, make me fall, tumble into our old passions. I wanted him to hold me and reassure me. 'Bye,' I said, and before I had the chance to say anything else, I cut the line.

E.J. Morrison

Fine Motor Skills

Though early for her, Janice was, of course, late. She was someone who even after ten years of living in the capital city *never* factored in the delays of London traffic. In her head, everything was a mere fifteen minutes away. And at four in the morning she was probably right. But she always drove in the day. In Janice's world it was: into the car - and off you go. She forgot the countless dustcarts, road-works, temporary stop lights, uncertain tourists not knowing you had to line up nose-to-tail to get through unfeasibly short red-to-green light changes, parades of military horses going to their exercises on some open space AND the gridlocked knock-on effects of a traffic accident two miles away. Today she was a mere fifteen minutes late, for the simple reason she got her times muddled up and set out half an hour earlier than the requirement.

But this had not saved Dora who had been waiting under the allocated lamp post at the appointed hour. She was soaked. She was standing in the sort of rain, usual for northern England and anywhere with a Celtic heritage, that was now becoming more common in London. A steady downpour that just kept on giving in its wet way.

Janice pulled up in her two-door Panda and reached over to open the passenger side.

'Op in,' she said. She was an unreconstructed Northerner. 'Or squelch in, more like.' She went on. 'Look at yuh! Loockih it's all a bit waterproof in ere'. She patted her faux-leather plastic seating.

Dora was drenched. She hadn't quite comes to terms with the way in which you kept having to wear different types of clothes for different reasons in different weathers. And this small grey island was a place of *many* different weathers. Today it was rain. And here she was in fleecy cotton track-suit bottoms, a cotton vest and an alpaca jumper that had doubled its weight. The tops of her cotton plimsolls were flattened with water and the latex soles acted as small sloshy, buckets to hold it.

And in spite of the proffered open door, Dora stood frozen, staring at it. She had never been in a car before and was unclear how best to approach getting from the street to the seat. Taking a deep breath, she lifted her right foot first and put it onto the car floor. But then, she was unsure which muscles to engage next. The best plan appeared to be to tip herself slightly backwards and try, limbo style, to get into the small car while gripping the sides for leverage. At least she knew that without doing this she would fall backwards and crack her head on the pavement. She paused half-way, aware of a sharp pain in her lower back and of her nose jammed against the door rim. Glancing at the passenger in the back who, from the view over her squashed nose, she could see only the knees and hands, Dora realised she had to end up facing the same way as the driver. If she carried on in this limbo-style entrance she'd end up sitting sideways with her legs on Janice.

Dora backed out and tried another tactic. She placed her knee on the seat, then the other knee, and spun round, but ended up *facing* the rather bemused woman in the back of the car.

'Errm, 'ave yuh got knee problems?' interrupted Janice sympathetically. 'You're like my gran. Do you want an 'and?'

Dora smiled and nodded; she'd seen that's what people did at moments like this, but said nothing. As it was a smile that didn't quite reach her eyes, which were now darting from side to side to try and judge the situation, she looked odd. The woman in the back seemed to be trying to suppress a feeling of growing alarm.

''Anggon... Terr-ih?...' Janice addressed the meek-looking woman in the back who cleared her throat and said quietly, 'It's Terr-A, actually'.

'Oh, yeah. Sorrih. Yeah.' She immediately forgot and launched on. 'Pass uz mih brollih. I'll coom round tuh yuh, Dora. Ave you not got a brollih with yuh? Honestly, coomin from Manchester like ah do we were braught oop with em. Av always got one about mih puhrson somewhere.'

'Bro-llih,' computed Dora. Perhaps this was a special device to lever people into such vehicles. She was glad Janice had one and wished she'd known about them so she could have asked for one earlier.

Terra passed over the small tent with the leopard-print markings. Janice flicked it open and splashed round to the other side of the car. Dora remained kneeling on the seat, awaiting further instructions, hands gripping the head rest, her face still painted with the fathomless grin and rolling eyes. Terra was beginning to feel vaguely terrified and hoped this woman had brought whatever medication she needed to quell what were obviously some sort of attacks.

'Raaaght. Let's start again,' boomed Janice. 'Can. You. Get. Out. Okay?' Standing on the pavement on Dora's side shielding both herself and the doorway from more rain, she punctuated her words as if communicating with one of her geriatric patients.

Dora reversed what she'd done on the way into the car and managed to get out quite speedily, at which point she realised that the 'brollih' was in fact a rain shield.

Terra had obviously been holding her breath, which now came out in a huge gasps through tense lips. Dora wondered why this should be.

'Raaaght', said Janice. 'Let's try again. Which knee is it?' By now the two women were crouching nose-to-nose outside the car, shoulders touching under the shelter of the umbrella. Most humans would have found this close proximity unnerving but Janice was used to being intimate with patients. And Dora was an alien.

'It's the left woon, intit? Raaaght. So keep facing me, grab mih and, and lower yourself, bum first.' Dora wasn't sure what the instruction was but started sitting down. Janice could feel her transferring weight and realised just in time she hadn't made any adjustments to lower her head and it was about to crash painfully into the door frame.

'Oo, anggon. Anggon,' she raised her pitch. 'Raaaght. Is it your neck as well?'

At this point, Dora had *utterly* no clue what was happening and decided the best course of action was to continue nodding.

'Raaaght. So SLOW-LY, bend your neck towards me, now tip back.' She balanced the umbrella between her shoulder and the car so she could grip Dora's elbows with both hands.

'That's raaaght. Now you get your right leg in and *I'll* lift the other one in. OK-AY?'

Dora nodded and felt exhausted already. These three days might prove difficult in ways she hadn't imagined. But the task was at last accomplished.

'Oh crikey. Look. Yuh bag.' Janice scooped up a sodden canvas bag from the pavement that had changed from a pale to a dark grey. 'Mustn't forget that. I'll pop it in the boot.'

Then she ran back to the driver's seat and carefully slotted the dripping umbrella just behind her and away from Terra. 'I'm sure yuh don't want to share the wet love, do yuh, Terrih?' She beamed at Terra who was about to correct her name again but Janice had moved her attentions back to Dora.

'Raaaght. What are we going to do with you, then? You'll catch yuh death if you don't get out of them clothes. Annnd,' she stretched the word out, 'we won't be goin' nowhere coz of the steam,' and reached forward to flick on the de-mister.

'So let's get you ome for a quick change. Yuh near, aren't yuh?

Dora nodded. This was all logical. This woman was right. This cold, wet state was not good for a human. But she lived in a shed at the bottom of someone's garden. This was not right in human terms. They would ask questions.

She could buy some new clothes. No, she remembered how long it had taken her to source the ones she already had, and even in human form she was sure she would experience the same pain when she touched them.

'Yes. Thank you,' she said, thinking quickly. 'I will run in. You can wait in the car. No sense in us all getting wet?' - pleased she was employing what she thought of as human logic. It seemed to work.

She directed Janice to the road and they parked in front of the house. 'Anggon. Ah'll coom round and get yer out,' beamed the generous Janice.

Dora thought for a moment. She'd now processed which muscle groups she needed to engage to do this complex task. 'No... I'll... be fine... now,' she said haltingly. 'Sometimes... it's... okay.'

'Well, take the brollih, at least.' Janice grabbed it from behind her with such a horizontal flourish that if Terra had not moved fast, the point would have caught her left nostril and ripped it open.

Dora discharged herself nimbly from the car, wrestling with the mysteriously unopenable umbrella and went off to change.

'D'ye think shiz foreign or on antidepressants or summat? She's a bit funnih, int shi? Takes all sorts, ah spawz,' mused Janice to Terra before launching forth on her views on the merits of yogurt and wound control.

Dora returned speedily in dry clothes, pleased that in the time she'd spent away from them she worked out how to get the umbrella up and down.

They set off. Janice liked to talk; she was not the sort that needed an answer, but she *did* like an audience. And two quiet women, even if a bit odd, captive in her car on the four-hour trip to Shropshire, were perfect fodder.

Dora tried at first to keep up and give answers, but following the lead of the woman in the back, soon realised that the occasional noise appropriate to the topic was all that was required. A tutting sound and shaking of the head when Janice lowered her voice and said something was terrible – 'shockin' was the word she liked to use a lot. And a little 'aha' of agreement every now and then. Subjects included the state of the NHS, which Janice had just left; how big *is* a big arse – Danny, her boyfriend, who she managed to fit into most topics, apparently liked something to hold on to; a diatribe about dieting; and an hour on the benefits of home delivery over supermarket shopping.

At several points, Dora found herself drifting into the sleep world. She was just about getting used to this state, but still had to check that she wasn't transforming inappropriately.

It was while in one on these half-waking, half-sleeping states that she and the dashboard seemed to move together rapidly. It all happened in a tumble of senses. A bang, a jerk, a tug, a bounce of her head forwards, a bounce of it back against the head-rest, a shriek blending seamlessly into mangled words from Janice, a high-pitched cry from Terra and another human voice – her own – letting out a grunt formed somewhere at the back of her throat, and that same rush of hormones she'd felt when she'd nearly been strangled. The fight-or-flight juices... but who was she going to fight? And, strapped into a metal box, she couldn't flee.

She moved her hand over the ridges of the seat-belt and re-alised she was experiencing a sharp stab of pain on inhaling - on her left side, just where the safety belt skimmed under her breast. She felt... she wasn't sure what it was, but she didn't like it. Having never been in pain before she had nothing to gauge it against. It felt severe, and it was in one place. It happened when she inhaled. For the first time, she consciously thought about this act of breathing. Other than that initial donning of her body, she hadn't given it a second thought, one of the myriad of autonomic systems that people only thought about when they went wrong.

While Dora rifled through all this new information, Janice un-buckled her belt and leapt out of the car into the now light drizzle. In the great scheme of car accidents it couldn't get more minor than this. They were jammed in single file between two lines of orange and white cones, bumper-to-bumper with the drivers of vehicles who were equally worn down by the drudgery of their stop-start journey. The three lanes on the other side were sailing by and Janice had momentarily, mentally, gone over to that moving side and had gently pressed the accelerator. The man in front hadn't made that same journey. Hence the small crunch.

Janice was staring at the broken headlight and dented registration plate. She was biting her lip and saying to no one in particular, 'Oh Dannih. He's goin to behead mih.'

'Are you okay?' Terra asked Dora.

'Yes, no, yes, no.' replied Dora. 'Pain in ribs where seat band was. My breath is sore.'

'Oh – we must get Janice to see you. She *is* a nurse'.

Dora looked out of the window where Janice was distorting her face with over-articulated vowels and miming over-sized pens writing on invisible giant paper to a blank-looking man. So many types of human behaviour. So little time to discover them.

Barbara Wren

Words Made Flesh

MEN WHO HAD LOVED HER ONCE READ THIS SHORT STORY SHE'D HAD PUBLISHED and wondered whether that fella in it was themselves. It was flattering and frightening at the same time. Exhilarating and a little bit creepy. 'This bit could be me,' they thought, 'but that bit... ah, no. Though... looked at differently and filed under "interesting" maybe that fella *could* be me.'

She'd won a competition for a short story she'd written and got it published in *The Irish Times*. The Arts page. Under a picture of a leaf. Great, big, green fronds spilling out into her story, dipping into the text, almost knocking it off the page.

'What's that about?' she thought when she first saw it. She was inspecting the various copies she'd spread out on her bed to admire (with disbelief) her first published piece. 'Is that a leaf in there? What's that leaf for? Who put a great big, green leaf right in the middle of my story?'

She bought four copies for herself and then they started arriving in the post from family and friends in Ireland. As if maybe she'd missed it – been busy that day, or something. Her mother's copy arrived first with a card saying 'Congratulations on Passing Your Exam!' Inside she'd written 'It was the nearest thing I could find.' Her mother rang to congratulate her. She was proud, you could hear it in her voice – at last she'd done something worthwhile. 'The number of people who've been asking me this week – is that your daughter?' her voice beamed down the phone and the line stretching out under the Irish Sea trailed the unspoken echo 'at last.... yes, at last... That's my girl.' She hadn't read it though. 'Ah, no love, it's not my thing, but it looks great. I liked the leaf.'

But the men read it. One review said: *a glorious distinctive voice, subverting eroticism, it creates a new, darker sexuality from everyday encounters...* So the men read it for the dirty bits. And wondered who that fella was.

A girl she'd been to college with had written a novel that began with sex. The first line was like those descriptions teenagers spend hours searching for, and returning to, in trashy books. It wasn't a trashy story though, just a good, shocking start. She'd followed the girl's career thoughtfully (main thought: I could do that). Sex seemed like a good beginning. Promising, she said to herself. And looked at from another angle, wasn't it the beginning of every-thing that mattered? And dirty, meaningful, and pleasing all in one go – what could be better for her story with a difference? Remak-ing the same story again and again with feeling – that's what sex could be on a good day. She thought that she'd give it a go.

Before she got it finished the girl who wrote the novel had a prize-winning short story published. This was a clever story, too – clever in both heart and mind – making you wrestle with some-thing. Leaving you feeling unexpectedly different by the end, as if sediment had settled gently inside you, in a dark, rusty place you hadn't visited for a while.

In this prize-winning story, a woman coped with the imminent death of her mother by having adulterous, rough sex with a man she slightly despised. 'File me under interesting, but not despised.' Did some male readers think that when they read the story? The two themes – clumsy, false beginnings and the end of life – col-lided violently, cleverly, passionately in a story that was shock-ingly disrespectful to mothers and their passing. How else could it be? Sometimes violent acts are necessary in the face of impossible losses, she thought, when she read it.

Her mother sent her a copy of the story: 'You remember that girl who was in your class in college, the one that's done very well for herself, well, she's won a competition – I've sent you the story.'

After she'd read it, making (mental) notes all the while and stopping sometimes to contemplate the loss of her own mother and just what kind of sex might be needed to obliterate that, she started to write a story of her own. She thought of a starting point, she thought of the structure, she thought of some characters. Her mind wandered. She thought of dark, red wine trickling out from the side of her mouth, the feel and the smell of it on her skin. 'How do you put tasting on the page?' she asked herself. The phone rang. 'Did you read that story before you sent it?' she asked her mother. 'Ah, no love, it's not my thing. I know a lot of my friends didn't like it, though.'

The fella she was going out with asked her what she was scribbling at, and if he could have a look. She'd heard somewhere that you should never show something till it's finished. Otherwise it was like letting the sun on an undeveloped film – the picture gets ruined, can't hold any colour or light. Plus, she was afraid she'd lose her voice, forget what she wanted to say, especially if he made a suggestion.

'Not a suggestion, please God, not a suggestion!' she teased as he raised his eyebrows – smiled and frowned while he read. She was never able to say no to him.

'I'm saying nothing,' he said. 'Nothing!'

'I'd appreciate that,' she said.

'I'll just say one thing, though – we've never done it like that.' He poured her a glass of red wine, his eyebrow still raised.

Edit, edit and then edit again. She'd read this in her creative writing handbook. She was sitting at her desk, pretending that her pen was a fine-toothed comb. Sort the wheat from the chaff. First you get the putty then you sculpt. Off you go.

Outside, the city was waking. She looked out of the window and tried to describe it, imagining that the rain hitting the window and sliding down to the sill was on her skin. She was the glass, and she could feel the movement of the rain, the heat of her body taking the sting and the speed out of it. She was watching the way the water moved, some straight lines, some blurred, some just drops disappearing into nowhere.

'How do I describe that?' she thought. 'The way water just ends.'

Her mother rang one morning when she was half-way through her story. That was what she'd started to say to herself. 'I am midway through my story today.' She would say it out loud to the kettle as she made their coffee. (She was reading a book called *Get a (Writing) Life: Believe YOU can.......do IT*). 'Before I started that book,' she thought, 'I would have said "I'll never finish this bloody story."'

'What are you doing in that writing group at all?' her mother said. 'Do you know Bertie Ahern's daughter has just had her second novel published? She's 22 and got a one million advance for her first. How's George?'

'Jorge, Mum. His name's Jorge, he's from Frankfurt.'

'Jorge, George, whatever - how is he? Has he got a permanent contract yet?'

'He's fine, Ma.'

He was fine. Very fine. He was lying right beside her looking a bit tired. But very fine. 'Well, maybe we've never done it like that before, but that's no reason we can't do it now,' was the last thing he'd said.

It seemed like a long time ago now. He didn't like to speak afterwards and she did. Maybe that was why she'd answered the phone. And now, because she had, she was lying in bed naked and tangled with him talking to her mother about Bertie Ahern's daughter.

'I'm saying nothing,' he said when she got off the phone.

Later that day, the fella who had broken her heart rang her up.

'Hello you,' he said. As if it wasn't three years since they'd spoken. As if there hadn't been all that time, those tears, to shed half the skin he'd once loved. Hello you. The shocking intimacy of calling me you, she thought to herself. 'That was me, wasn't it?' he said, 'that fella who liked it in the bath?' She was drawing circles on her desk as he spoke. Spirals of blue ink stained the desk then fanned out wetly, seeping into the stark, naked, empty pages. This ink has a life of its own, she thought, watching it filling in all the blank spaces.

'I always knew you had it in you!' he said.

Honestly, she thought, putting down the phone and throwing his new mobile number in the bin. Honestly, you couldn't make him up. Her fella said, 'Not that way. Do it like this. Smoothly, softly.

Don't be rough, be gentle.' She was at the window. He, and all the words and the room itself spread out behind her. She thought of strong words, the rough energy of them. The making of them. She thought about gentleness. She imagined love as a knife and a feather carving and soothing flesh. 'Shape and meaning,' she told her fella. 'I need more shape and meaning in this story.'

A man who had known her a long time ago rang and asked if she'd meet him for a cup of tea. 'God, you've taken me back in time,' he said. 'That story, the things we used to do to each other. It all came racing back. Those were great days, weren't they?' As he spoke a pigeon took off from her window ledge and she tracked its flight with her finger along the streaked glass. She listened to him and remembered a freckle he'd had at the top of his leg and a song he once made up for her and danced to with no clothes on. And the way his eyes never said the same thing as his mouth.

'I haven't been able to stop thinking about that time since I read your piece,' he said. 'God, those were the days!' and he was off, remembering, as she dropped her hand and watched the pigeon fly out of view. Why is it, she thought, letting him ramble on, that stories seem so much clearer on the page? Clearer than memory could ever be. They are what they are. A feeling that you have at the end tells you that a story has finished and settled within your skin. That's what it was, you say to yourself, a story. Life, on the other hand, leaves you gasping all the time, wondering, 'but what was that?' A story has a shape and colour. Life is more like a leaky vase, spraying bits of old daffodils, the odd wild rose, pollen stains on your nose, and water that always gets you in all the wrong places. And still he was speaking. 'God, it was great, wasn't it? What was it that we had between us then? It was electric.' She began to wonder if he was a bit jarred.

'What indeed?' she thought. 'Who could say now?'

'I can't believe how long it's been. It would be great to catch up. Just as a friend, like,' he said when she hesitated. 'What could be wrong with that? A quick cup of tea tomorrow.'

After she hung up she sat for a long time watching the city through her window, seeing the light change, and her own feelings come and go like colours she could sculpt just momentarily until time put them in the shade. 'A quick cup of tea,' she said to herself, glad to be safe in the house, hugging her glass of wine, the warm redness of it, the glow of memory it made, until it seemed to swell up in her blood and surge right through her.

Her mother went on holiday. 'The sun in winter... it's the only way to go,' she said before she swanned off to Marrakesh. She was taking three books with her. 'I might have to give it a go,' she said, 'that book by Bertie Ahern's daughter. It'll be at the airport. I'm on my holidays. Don't want anything too heavy.'

She kept in touch by text. 'Touched down,' came the first message and always the weather in capitals FREEZING or SUN SHINING... at last! 'Sunshine in January,' she thought when she got the texts. 'It's a bit of a risk.' When everyone had stopped sending her copies of her own story, she took one of the *Irish Times*' to the park to read it alone in the sunshine. She thought she'd read all the articles on the page before and after her piece. As if they were preserving agents, with her story held in time between them. The date above and page numbers below, forever. These pages with their numbers and dates, and this park that she loved, the green hard earth of it, would be where her piece first saw the light of day.

Some day it will be archived, she thought, a little bit grandly now that she had fourteen copies of it. Black print, white paper – maybe yellowing – will be curling into itself. She'd decided to overlook the leaf - and modern technology while she was at it. She imagined it filed in that library in Dublin where once she'd sat wordless, dreamlike, just waiting. She held the paper against her face and smelled its mustiness. The ink and the paper felt more substantial than she did. 'I'm published, Ma,' she said to herself, sending light words across a winter park at dusk. 'All this time I've

been doing it in the dark and now I've got it down on the page.'
The paper crackled warmly against her skin.

He had left her story on the bedside table after he read it – from the
bed she could see the green leaf behind him, spilling out onto the
text. He was on his side – his head in one of his hands, her breast in
the other. She had forgotten the strength in his hands, the sureness
of him. His hands, her skin, He moved towards her and she watched
him closely, matching him breath for breath, She remembered this.
His hands, her skin. His skin. All of him. So close now she couldn't
see him. Up close blocking out the light. The leaf was gone into the
shadows, the text bleeding off the page. The words were inside her
now – he was inside her. Beyond words, beyond sight, beyond skin
now. She started breathing again. *It was me, it was me, it was me,
it was always me,* he was saying. *It was me.* But in the dark it could
have been any of them, making the leaf spin, and the words fly
away, and her flesh grab out until the silence screamed. The story
began again.

Biographies

Meera Ashish is a columnist and travel journalist writing for international publications. She hops between different continents every fortnight and during her travels, has written her first novel, which draws on the experiences of a British Indian girl trying to deal with and ultimately merge her two identities. Born and brought up in London, Meera now lives in Dubai and East Africa.

Laurika Bretherton is a freelance writer who has lived in Namibia, South Africa and Chicago before making London her home. She's currently working on her first novel set in South Africa in 1994, a time filled with suspicion, resentment and hope. She married her childhood sweetheart, and when she's stressed, she bakes cookies.

Janet Colson had a career as one of London's leading arts fund-raisers when she started writing fiction and poetry. "Patrick's Place" is an extract from her first novel, *The Story She Told Herself*, about a woman's journey through loss to self-discovery, set in French Manhattan and Cape Cod. She is married and has a young son.

Isla Dunham is an Oxford graduate and an award-winning journalist who has written for a broad range of publications including *The Economist*, *The Telegraph* and *Harper's and Queen*. From 1991, she spent ten years working as a journalist and living in Asia. In December 2004, she survived the tsunami while on holiday in Sri Lanka and this led her to set up a school there for street children. Currently, she divides her time between her family, managing the school in Sri Lanka and writing her first novel. She lives in London.

Rosemary Furber's novel *The Most Intimate Place* was published last summer by the Maia Press, following *What You See Is What You Get*, a ghost novel for the 10-14 age group, published in 2005. Both are set in Greenwich and Blackheath where she has lived with her family for 25 years.

Tree Garnett grew up between the Highlands of Scotland, London and the South of France. She read English Literature at Oxford University, has made TV drama series and worked as a psychoanalyst. She lives in West London and has four children.

Rochelle Gosling was born in South Africa and now lives in London with her husband and two young sons. Previously a news journalist and then European Head of Communications for a major global corporation, she has travelled extensively and is passionate about the African continent.

David S. Hickson is a one-time new media lawyer, now internet entrepreneur. His writing style has been described as 'existential gothic' which he rather likes despite not knowing what it means. He is working on his fourth novel.

Atalanta Miller studied English Literature at Oxford University and is currently working in shipping. She has been writing short stories and poems since she could read and is finally writing her first novel. She lives in London with her husband, three children, two dogs and her many, many books.

Peter Miller is a freelance translator and subtitler. He is currently working on his second novel. He has previously had work published in the fanzine Papercuts and on the literary website Badosa. com. Peter lives in Maidenhead with his wife and daughter.

E.J. Morrison has been planning a book since the age of seven. Several decades on she has now run out of excuses not to do it.

Distractions from her writing include her work as a voice coach with actors, journalists and business people.

Jennifer Nadel is a qualified barrister and award-winning journalist who has reported for the BBC, Channel Four News and ITN from around the world. Her first book *Sara Thornton: The Story of a Woman Who Killed* was published by Gollancz and made into a film by the BBC and a documentary by Channel 4. She is now concentrating on her first work of fiction - a collection of short stories. She lives in London with her husband, three sons and two dogs.

Susan Oke has worked in teaching and development within the Further and Higher Education sectors in both West Africa and the UK. Her experience of the tensions between different cultures and religions is reflected in her first novel set in an alternative world of telepaths.

Gerda Pearce was born in Mthatha, South Africa, and was educated in the Eastern Cape and at Rhodes University. She worked as a hospital pharmacist in Cape Town and Namibia before moving to Britain where she worked as an osteopath. She is now a writer and editor and lives in Notting Hill. Her first novel, *Long Lies the Shadow*, is published by Maia/Arcadia in 2011.

Mark Pendry is the Commercial Director for a Apple Support company. He lets out his creative side at evenings and weekends by acting, playing in a band, and, of course, writing. He has completed a play and a number of short stories and is currently working on his first novel.

Rosie Rowell is South African. She came to London on a short working holiday in 2003 with a backpack and a pair of hiking boots. Eight years later she is still in London, has since lost the backpack but gained a husband and three small children. The hiking boots remain unused. She is completing her first novel about growing up in a small town in South Africa.

Sarah Sotheron has set up several successful companies, most recently in the hotel industry. She is the winner of a short story competition and has written several radio plays. Currently she is working on her first novel set in the Second World War.

Colette Swires, after completing her masters at Sotheby's Institute, wrote for several art magazines before going on to work at a London auction house where she had the idea for her first novel, *Never Say Neville Again.*

Roderic Vincent is a Chartered Psychologist. His stories have been shortlisted for the Aesthetica Award and the Bridport Prize. Two of his poems are anthologised in *The Iron Book of New Humorous Verse*. He is currently looking for representation for his second novel. He blogs as part of the team at strictlywriting.blogspot.com

Julia Weetman grew up in Asia and now lives in Brussels with her husband and a recidivist Jack Russell. She is working on her first novel, which is based in Hong Kong and China during the lead up to the Tiananmen Square massacre.

Barbara Wren is a psychologist and a writer. She has written for Cara magazine, and the Guardian and two of her short stories were shortlisted for the Fish Short Story competition in 2010. She is currently working on a novel *Fragments: A Love Story*, and a collection of short stories.

Editor Biographies

Maggie Hamand is a journalist, non-fiction author and novelist. She was the winner of the first World One-Day Novel cup and her winning novel, *The Resurrection of the Body*, was first published by Michael Joseph and has been recently optioned for film. Her second novel, *The Rocket Man*, has also been published, along with several short stories, some of which have been shortlisted for prizes. She taught novel writing at Morley College, was Writer in Residence at Holloway Prison, London, and a Royal Literary Fund Fellow at London University of the Arts. She founded and directed the acclaimed small independent publisher The Maia Press (now part of Arcadia Books) and has recently published the definitive guide for beginner writers, *Creative Writing For Dummies*.

Shaun Levin is the author, most recently, of *Trees at a Sanatorium* and *Snapshots of The Boy*. His other books include *Seven Sweet Things* and *A Year of Two Summers*. His short stories appear in anthologies as diverse as *Between Men, Modern South African Stories, Boyfriends from Hell* and *The Slow Mirror: New Fiction by Jewish Writers*. He is the founding editor of *Chroma*, a queer literary and arts journal.

Natalie Butlin studied English Literature and went on to do a Masters in Creative Writing at the University of East Anglia. She has worked at the literary charity First Story and as an intern at Random House Children's Books, Transworld, the Poetry Society and literary agents Johnson & Alcock. She has run adult and children's writing workshops at UEA and in a variety of other settings. She writes short fiction.